MW01249266

Dear Readers

As you probably already know, I like to challenge myself every three years and do something new in my writing career. That's the reason the new Diamonds of London series was born.

In this series, you'll find feisty, determined heroines who aren't content with the status quo, so they'll fight to have the lives — and loves — they truly deserve. Of course, the heroes they choose are endearing, sexy, strong, and oh-so-swoon worthy! Another key thing to note is the fact that many of the books in this series will take place outside of London as well as beyond England. Believe it or not, life *did* happen elsewhere during the Regency period. ▨

I hope you enjoy *My Dear Mr. Ridley*. I've waited a very long time indeed for this book — and this series — to launch. I hope, as well, you fall in love with this new couple.

Happy reading!

Sandra

Dedication

To Paula Peppers. Thank you for always supporting me and for making me smile every time I scroll through Facebook and see your posts. I wish you nothing but luck and happiness in your future!

Acknowledgements

Thanks for offering up names for Mr. Ridley's cat.

Paula Shackelford Peppers, Amy O'neal
Nicole Atkeson, Michelle Fidler
Belinda Wiley Wilson, Shawn Dalton-Smith
Kat Tolle, Cecilia R. Rodriguez
Kathleen Garley, Donna Antonio
Faith Kirk, Mary Vinecore
Marsha Lambert, Nancy Hardy
Angela Pryce, KJ Montgomery
Patricia Way, Dorothy Callahan
Sara Lopiccolo, Angie Eads
Tana Hillman, Jennifer Morin
Darleen Perez, Miranda Pelham
Jennifer Lynn Green-Prescott
Santa O'Byrne, Hanny Van de Kamp
Tina Brower Medlock, Glenys O'Connell
Janice Seagraves, Rachel E. Moniz
Jayne Smith, Gloria E. Trinidad-Tellez
Beth Hinterleiter-Udall, Marcelle Cole
Sharon Villone Doucett, Julie McDonough
Sally Brandle, Janis Susan May
Christine Warner

Blurb

Sometimes, the road to romance is littered with intrigue, harrowing danger, and wild shock.

The year is 1818 and Theodosia Netherton—Lady Ballantyne—is wintering in the sunny climes of Italy in an effort to protect her health as well as to visit her brother. Widowed for three years, she has no interest in a new romance, but when a horrific emergency leads her to the doorstep of a handsome, former Bow Street Runner with wide shoulders and a mysterious scar, she might just change her mind.

Mr. Hudson Ridley is in Rome for the warmth and relative obscurity. Retired at the age of eight and thirty, the last thing he wants is to become embroiled in a kidnapping plot that involves an attractive widow and her missing son. Yet he was the best in the retrieval business in his prime, and she did have hauntingly unforgettable eyes as well as a smile that could make a man do wicked, stupid things.

In the quest to hunt the people who nabbed the boy and heir to a viscounty, Theodosia and Hudson dance about mutual desire until passion gets the better of them one star-lit evening amidst some of the country's finest ruins. But tracking the criminals turns deadly when shots are fired at them. Time is running out to rescue the young heir, keep a valuable jewel safe, and somehow discover if love is the ultimate reward despite the risk.

Can two fearful hearts feel less broken together? Find out in My Dear Mr. Ridley, the first book in the exciting new Diamonds of London series.

Chapter One

May 8, 1818
Minerva Villa
Rome

"I shall never tire of admiring the beauty found here," Theodosia Netherton—Lady Ballantyne—murmured to her maid, Doris. "The fact there is so much sunshine and the scent of flowers on the breezes simply astounds me." Even the name of her brother's villa in Rome was charming.

Minerva was the Roman goddess of wisdom, justice, law, victory, and the sponsor of arts, trade, and strategy. She was not a patron of violence such as the God Mars, but of *strategic* war, of intelligence and no doubt diplomacy. The name was fitting for an ambassador's residence, and since Thomas was the English ambassador to Rome, it was nothing except perfect.

The maid chuckled as she went about the light and airy bedchamber tidying up clothing. "My lady, you have been here for four months already. Surely you have acclimated by now."

"Not a bit of it. Every day is seemingly a miracle after everything else." Theodosia smiled when the sound of enthusiastic child laughter wafted up from the courtyard below. Her son was enjoying the company of a few other boys his age, which made her happy, for he needed that interaction. "Beyond that, I am heartily enjoying myself while in Rome."

Already, she'd toured the city, but she suspected there was so much more to see than the usual tourist things and churches her guides had shown her. What she really wanted to do was tramp beneath the streets, poke about into the hidden places that really contained history, walk where leaders had tread and perhaps see treasures that human eyes hadn't seen for centuries.

"I'd say you don't wish to return to London."

"Mmm. Perhaps for a variety of reasons."

Was that true? Perhaps, but then, there was nothing wrong with that decision for being a widow for nearly three years and feeling that mourning had been quite a change. While in England, she'd been beset with memories and had been stuck in an emotional quagmire that had followed the death of her husband—

Viscount Ballantyne. The secrets they had kept as a couple were now overwhelming, and she'd been so tired in remaining strong for her eight-year-old son Jacob. Without her husband's protection, old fears had crept back into her life to the point that she felt like breaking. When her brother had written and invited her to spend some time with him at his ambassador's residence, she'd accepted with alacrity.

It was time for a change. *I am ready to be happy again, ready to look forward to things again.* Would that include a new courtship or marriage? She didn't know in this moment, but something different would be welcome.

"However, a lady cannot remain in mourning forever. I welcome returning to wearing gowns in more lively colors."

"Oh, that reminds me. Your modiste had two of her seamstresses deliver new gowns and other clothing you ordered las week. I am having them pressed as we speak."

"Ah, lovely. I cannot wait to wear them." A faint smile curved her lips. "You must admit, though, this climate has been good for my health." Away from dirty, polluted London, her lungs didn't hurt as much when she breathed, and her nose wasn't as stuffy. Would that she could remain in Rome for an extended visit, and she just might, for it wasn't essential Jacob return to London in order to take up the reins of the viscounty just yet.

"There is that." Doris paused near Theodosia's spot on the balcony. "I am glad your health has improved. There is far too much sickness in London already without struggling over breathing problems."

"Indeed." Such things had always plagued her, but she'd been wildly happy in her formative years. Her parents had been attentive and loving; everything she'd wished to have in her own marriage. "I remember being sickly as a child. Only when we went to Papa's country estate did I have a reprieve."

"You are certainly brighter in Rome. Not so sad, I think."

"This is true." A sigh escaped Theodosia. "As much as I miss Nathaniel, I am quite certain he wouldn't have wished for me to live the remainder of my days as a widow wringing my hands and wearing mourning or never indulging in anything fun."

Having attained her twenty-eighth year and being a widow for three years, she'd come to a better understanding of herself. Perhaps her weak lungs had a better chance of feeling halfway decent in warmer, drier climates, but such a lovely backdrop hadn't managed to fully heal her broken heart. Oh, she'd loved Nathaniel—perhaps to distraction—but wasn't that the point of love? She'd married the viscount after a whirlwind courtship when she was but nineteen, and he'd surely turned her head during her Come Out year, and since then, he had been her best friend, her lover, her sounding board and constant companion. Six years with him hadn't been enough time.

Losing him—and quite violently at that—had left a gaping hole in her life that nothing had been able to fill thus far. She would never forgive fate for taking him away so soon, but truthfully, she wished to feel whole again.

"Lord Ballantyne was a good man, this is true," Doris said in a soft voice as she folded a cashmere wrap of Theodosia's. "He doted on you. Never have I seen such love, but you are correct, my lady. He would wish for you live your life and find happiness again."

Slowly, Theodosia nodded. Doris had been with her since her marriage, so she had seen how Nathaniel had been. "Especially for Jacob's sake," she added quietly as she gazed across the sun-drenched courtyard where her son and his friends were playing in the afternoon's warmth. "I want him to use my marriage as a benchmark for the day when he wishes to find a bride."

"There is time enough for that. He is a boy yet. Let him enjoy his childhood before responsibilities intrude."

"Oh, he is." Even now, peals of laughter rang out across the courtyard as the boys kicked around a ball.

"Good."

"I am considering remaining in Rome for another year or so. Surely, I can easily hire a governess or tutors to take care of his schooling until we return."

"You can do whatever you would like, my lady." Doris clucked much like a mother hen. "Perhaps you should pursue marrying again. You are still beautiful and were a Diamond of the First Water in your youth. Those looks haven't faded."

The heat of embarrassment went through Theodosia's cheeks as she turned to peer at her maid. "I think you embellish too much." But the assessment pleased her. "I suppose I don't look too bad."

"I should say not if dark eyed, hot blooded men make suggestions whenever you go out." There was a bit of mischief in the maid's eyes. "Some of them have been quite blatant."

"Indeed." The heat in Theodosia's cheeks intensified. "Perhaps it is the novelty of seeing a blonde Englishwoman." But the vain part of her appreciated their notice. It had been a long time indeed since she'd received any sort of male attention. "Yet I am not searching for a Roman man since I must return to London eventually."

"Do you assume there are only natives in Rome?" Doris snorted as she went back inside the bedchamber.

"Of course not. However, from what I have seen of my fellow countrymen, they are either too old, have too much of a paunch, or are only searching for a tryst."

"As if a tryst wouldn't be good for you."

Shock went through Theodosia. "I want a man for more than a mere bedding." As much as she'd enjoyed intimate relations with her husband, she didn't know if she could share such things with a man who wouldn't want her past that... or even a man she didn't know well.

"Then take the bedding and see where it might lead." The maid shot her a grin. "Stop declining the invitations your brother gives you. If you do not go to society functions, you will never meet anyone interesting or dashing. His reach as an ambassador goes wide, and many people have vied to gain his notice."

"Well, Thomas is no slouch in the looks department either." Older than her by a decade, he had yet to marry even though he'd been quite popular with the ladies. "I think he rather enjoys bachelorhood too much." She peered once more into the courtyard. For the time being, the gay laughter and enthusiastic shouting had ceased.

The boys were clustered together around Jacob, who held something in his hand she couldn't quite see, but there was a brilliant flash of green before he put whatever it was into his waistcoat pocket. Then the knot disbursed, and the boys once more called to each other and again the ball was put into play.

"Yes, I for one am not concerned with the ambassador's marital prospects." Doris bustled to a clothes press. She tugged out a navy silk gown that sparkled with spangles and glass beads. "This will do nicely for his dinner party tonight, and you will have all eyes on you, I think."

"It's a beautiful piece." It thrilled her soul to dress in lovely clothing that made her feel all too feminine. "And perhaps just the thing to lift me out of the doldrums I've slipped into."

"I will make sure the wrinkles are pressed out. There is a pair of silver slippers that will go nicely with it, and perhaps we will thread silver ribbon in your hair tonight."

"Whatever you decide will be lovely." Theodosia glanced about her apartment and sighed with appreciation. "I really should seek Thomas out and ask him about the guests attending the dinner party tonight." Perhaps she would recognize a name or two.

"Very well." Doris laid the sparkling gown across the four-poster bed.

"Did I just hear my name in passing?" Her brother poked his head into the bedchamber since her door had been left partially open. "I was just on my way downstairs. Is all well?"

Theodosia and Doris shared a chuckle. "Of course. We were discussing what I should wear to your dinner party is all."

Surprise lined his face. "Ah, does that mean you will actually attend this time?"

"Yes." She waved him in. For a man ten years her senior, he was still quite handsome. His blond hair, done in the latest style, made him a veritable Adonis, and dressed as he was in the first stare of fashion, he was never without a lady on his arm. Yet none of them had made a deep enough impression that he'd offered for them. "I have decided it is probably time to re-enter society and see what there is to find."

"I'm so pleased!" He closed the distance between them then bussed her cheek. "It has made me sad to see you lost these past years."

Theodosia frowned. "It wasn't that I was lost. More like I was in the midst of shock and now I'm in the mood for a change."

"To live again."

She snorted. "Well, I have Jacob to live for, so this is merely a wish to assuage curiosity, let's say." With a shrug, she moved back to the balcony and watched her son play with his friends. What in the world was so fascinating with that ball that they couldn't manage to leave it be? Her brother followed. "I am not certain what I want from my life now, but it cannot be what it is currently."

Not that she was bored. Far from it, and neither was she overly lonely. However, she did miss the closeness that being with a man had brought into her life, missed the solid warmth of a man's arms about her, missed the thrill of being kissed. Whether marriage would come from such a thing was anyone's guess, but she had to start somewhere.

"I am proud you have decided to make this change." When Jacob glanced upward, Thomas waved to him. The boy waved back and then returned to playing with the other children. "Jacob has made efficient use of his time here and seems quite at home." He slid a glance her way. "Perhaps the both of you could linger for an extended stay. It's lovely having family about."

"It is, rather." Theodosia sighed. "And yes, I have given that matter thought recently. Perhaps I will look into engaging a governess soon, if you don't mind hosting us for longer than you initially thought."

"I would be delighted, and you seem to be flourishing health wise here, so why not? Perhaps we can hire a music master for him and even a dance instructor."

"Are you sure he isn't too young for that?"

"Mama and Papa made me and Percy start learning the ways of the *ton* at that age. Why not your son?" Percy was their other brother, two years older than Thomas, and the current Viscount Everly. Since Thomas was the second son, he didn't need to worry about being groomed for the title, so he went the route of diplomacy over politics or the church. He grinned as he clasped his hands behind his back. "After we have both lost so much of our family over the years, it is good to have you and Jacob close."

"Agreed." A breath of relief left her throat when her son disappeared under one of the arches that shaded the walkway beneath the upper stories of the villa. "Perhaps I can host your dinner parties and other events in the future if all goes well tonight." It was more than she'd given him since she'd arrived, but it was time to shake off the old sadness and find something new.

"I would like that above all things."

"Unless, of course, you might wish to marry." She nudged him in the ribs with an elbow.

"Not until you do the same."

"Cheeky." But she laughed, and it felt good to do so. "Making a late start of it today?"

"A bit. I was up rather late last night with a difficult meeting, but eventually a compromise was reached." He pulled his pocket watch out. "Now, I'm afraid I have another meeting that is just as important in a quarter of an hour. No time for tea it seems."

"Then I will see you at dinner."

"Absolutely. There are a few gentlemen I would like to introduce you to. All very fine men," he added when she raised an eyebrow.

"Upstanding members of society, and all quite fitting for a lady of your station. Fear not." He trained his gray-blue eyes on her, so much like hers. "If fortune is with us, this year will bring us both a renewal of blessings. We are both due for some of those."

"We are." She patted his shoulder before he turned away. "I hope you have a productive meeting. I sometimes think you work too hard and keep too long of hours."

"Thank you, and you aren't wrong, but being an ambassador requires this from time to time."

Once her brother departed, Doris came back into the room. "There is a bit of heat rising this afternoon, my lady. Would you care for some lemonade?"

"That sounds lovely. It's almost time for tea regardless, so I shall call Jacob inside, so please bring the lemonade and tea things to the balcony off the morning room. I always adore the views from there. After that, I want to perhaps visit the Trevi fountain with him. He needs to start on his history in any event."

"Of course, my lady. I'll order the refreshments and have them sent there for you."

"Thank you, Doris. It will be lovely to have some down time this afternoon before the anxiety of the evening is upon me."

The maid tsked. "You will be the star of the night, just as you were in your youth."

"I don't know about that." But Theodosia smiled, nonetheless as she made her way to the morning room. It was one of her most favorite rooms in the villa and featured much of the same views as her bedchamber.

The light, airy space, done in pleasing shades of peach and moss green always made her feel at home and at peace. It was here she did most of her correspondence, and if she were to truly become her brother's hostess, where she would meet with the staff and plan upcoming events. A tiny niggle of excitement buzzed at the base of her spine, for she had dearly missed being a vital part of someone's life. Perhaps she might find purpose again over and above being a mother.

She tidied the room, stacked a few periodicals and fashion magazines on one of the low tables to make room for the tea service. Not long afterward, a footman brought in a silver tea tray, including two tall cut crystal glasses of lemonade. After thanking the man, Theodosia took a glass in each hand and then moved to the balcony off that room. There was a dear little table and two chairs—all made from white-painted wrought iron—where she planned to take tea. She glanced into the courtyard just as a rush of boys came swarming back into the space with the ever-present ball.

"Jacob? Please join me upstairs. It's time for tea."

There was no answer in her son's sweet voice.

With a frown, Theodosia leaned a bit over the wrought iron railing of the balcony in order to see better, but there was no trace of him. "Jacob?" Cold fear twisted up her spine. *Oh, God.* Had it finally happened? Had her crime from years ago been found out at last? "Jacob! Where are you?"

One of the other boys, a dark-haired Italian lad, looked up at her with a hand shading his eyes. "He is not here, lady." He shrugged with all the elegance Italians inherently had. "He is gone now."

"Gone?" Panic filled her chest. The glasses of lemonade slipped from her suddenly lax fingers to shatter against the stonework at her feet. The cool liquid splashed over her ankles and toes, for she wore Roman-style sandals. "Gone where?"

"I do not know? He just… go." Then the boy returned to the knot of others, and they continued to play with their ball.

"Jacob!" The urge to retch climbed her throat, for old fears were coming home to roost even though she and her husband had been so terribly careful. Perhaps that wasn't it at all, but instead her son had wandered off. "Jacob!" Yet there was no sign of the boy, and she knew deep in her heart this was the beginning of the end.

Slowly, Theodosia sank to her knees as the strength left her body. "Jacob!"

Her screams came back to her in mocking echoes then she covered her face in her hands and let tears have at her.

Chapter Two

May 8, 1818
Mrs. Claudian's boarding house
Rome

Mr. Hudson Ridley sat on his favorite comfortable chair with his booted feet propped on a matching brocade ottoman. Months ago, he'd dragged the furniture out onto his balcony at the boarding house where he resided. It didn't matter to him the pieces didn't belong outside or that their removal from one of his front rooms left a gaping hole in the arrangement. He liked what he liked, and the chair was sturdy enough for his large frame.

Besides the two front rooms—one as a formal parlor and one for a more informal living space like a drawing room—the apartment he rented had two bedrooms in the back. He, of course, occupied the larger of the pair. The other remained unused, or rather Luna had taken it over as her private abode. There was also a water closet of sorts, which was rather lavish for a man of his means, but he'd not once complained. It made for a rather tidy existence. Meals, when he took them at the boarding house, were shared in a communal dining room with other residents, for Mrs. Claudian was a superb cook.

As of yet, she hadn't scolded him regarding moving the furniture or for drinking more than he ought, so he would continue to do as he pleased.

The afternoon was another pearl in the string of gems he'd collected since arriving in Rome two years before. Mellow sunlight flooded the area, shining down on the building — or *insulae* meaning island because the multi-storied buildings rose like islands throughout the ancient city — that housed his rooms or apartment. In the courtyards and nearby piazzas, laughter of children and the general buzz of conversation wafted through the air to his ears. The ring of horses' hooves against the cobblestone streets and the rumble of the wheels provided a comfortable background for his afternoon nap, as did the subtle fragrance of ever-present bougainvillea vines that trailed over balcony railings and up the sides of brickwork. Their cheerful colors of vibrant pinks, muted purples, and roses provided much needed splashes of colors in what might be an otherwise drab and dun world.

A snort of laughter escaped him, for there were times when he'd imbibed in too much imported brandy when he waxed poetic about his life, but then, without the spirits, he probably wouldn't be able to tolerate his life... or the reasons therein.

He winced as the burn from the brandy hit his throat. No matter what, the life he'd found here in Rome was infinitely better than what he'd walked away from in London over two years before. A frown tugged at the corners of his mouth as his mind descended into memories.

Two and a half years ago, he'd been a principal officer with Bow Street, and the case he'd been on had been the greatest challenge of his career. One night, while in pursuit of his quarry, he'd been ambushed by a different criminal entirely. After an intense bout of fisticuffs, his opponent had pulled out a knife with a wickedly serrated blade, and since it had been dark and raining, Hudson hadn't seen the weapon in time to avoid it. The other man had lashed out and had carved his left cheek and temple. Since the cuts had gone deep, they'd left ugly scars, but beyond that, the injury — and the putting down of the knife-wielding man — had left him incapacitated enough that Hudson didn't catch his original case criminal, which meant that man had killed another innocent victim and made that murder number five.

As far as he knew, the case remained unsolved to this day, for after that night, Hudson had made the decision to leave Bow Street's service. He had been reprimanded by his superiors for his inability to catch the murderer — regardless of the countless cases he'd solved for Bow Street — and then he'd spent a few weeks recovering from his injuries. During that time, he'd thought about his career, took the unsolved case hard, and eventually resigned.

Wanting to put as much distance between himself and the scene of his greatest failure, Hudson had packed his belongings and then removed to the sunny, warm climes of Rome. While employed, he'd lived modestly and had managed to tuck away half his yearly salary each year since he'd began his career, so he was more well off than most when arriving in the Eternal City. It had taken next to no time to find the boarding house with its weird slightly leaning façade, but the location was close to everything he was interested in — sites, food, strolling the streets, entertainment — and he'd settled into his new life with alacrity.

A sneeze from close by wrenched him from those musings. He glanced over his shoulder and smiled at Luna, his closest companion. It didn't matter that she was a two-and-a-half-year-old feline. "Are you well?"

The white Persian sneezed again and then proceeded to lick one of her paws. She had one orange front paw and one orange back paw. There was also a tiny orange dot at the tip of her tail.

"Ah. Business as usual, then?"

Currently, Luna the cat was the only female he allowed into his life. One day shortly after he'd arrived in Rome, Hudson had found her wandering the Via del Corso. It was one of the main streets of the city, and since it dissected the center of the city, it was one of his favorite places to ramble. The rather long street hosted the famed Piazza del Popolo at the top end and at the bottom the Piazza Venezia.

One of his favorite places to visit was off that main street where the Piazza di Spagna was, with the Trevi Fountain on one side and the Pantheon on the other. It was here that he enjoyed sitting and perhaps sipping tea or coffee. At others, he partook of various vendors and their handcarts for his dinner and simply watched the people who came to gawk at the fountain. Occasionally, more adventurous ladies would wade into the waters of that fountain, and some of them had attractive calves indeed. Those were good days. On the bad ones, there was always the sunshine that reminded him he was still alive for a reason, and even if his scarring kept female companionship to a minimum and left him broken, he was part of a bigger whole.

In one of those alleys, he'd discovered a scrawny, hungry kitten who'd fought him tooth and nail when he'd scooped her up. Since it had been winter when he'd arrived in Rome, he'd worn a greatcoat at the time, and when he'd come upon the shivering feline, he'd merely tucked her into a pocket and brought her home with him.

She'd been his constant companion ever since. The name of Luna had come immediately to mind, for it had been under a full moon that he'd found her, and since she was mostly white, it made sense. Now, the cat was healthy and very well fed, and she was quite protective of him whenever anyone came to call—especially if that visitor was also a female—which amused him heartily.

Luna meowed. The cat jumped onto the ottoman, nudged one of his boots with her nose until he moved them, and proceeded to give herself a bath in the sunlight.

It was just easier to have a cat than to give his time to a human woman, and he was comfortable with that. The cat, though more than capable of judging him for a host of reasons, never did so because of his looks or his failings. Luna ruled his life and the rooms he rented, but everyone—including his landlady—adored her as well as her antics. Never had he seen a cat presented with as many treats as she was. Spoiled? Probably. Did she deserve it?

Absolutely. After spending the first months of her life on the streets, he would give her the world if the cat requested it.

Before he could let himself drift off for an afternoon nap, a peremptory knock sounded on his door. There was no opportunity to answer it, for the panel swung open and his matronly landlady came into the room.

Well, damn.

"Good afternoon, Mrs. Claudian." It was a regular occurrence for the woman to sail into his home without regard to boundaries or privacy. Because of that, he refused to clamber to his feet on principal. "How can I be of service?" Not that he would try very hard, for he wasn't in the habit of helping anyone these days.

There was no point to it.

"Such bad manners." The woman fairly clucked like a mother hen as she came to the door of the balcony. She tsked her tongue and gave him a friendly smack to the shoulder. "You are slovenly today."

By willpower alone, Hudson stopped himself from rolling his eyes. "What is wrong with being in my shirtsleeves when I am not planning to entertain or see anyone?" He eyed her askance. "Why are *you* here?" There was simply no point of being polite with her; she thought it her sworn duty to take care of him for whatever reason.

She huffed and rested her hands on her ample hips as he craned his neck to look up at her. "Rude." Though there was no censure in her expression, only fondness. "You shouldn't be alone."

"I am not alone. Luna is here." Hudson nodded to his cat who watched him with her bewitching golden eyes.

"How many times do I tell you a cat is not true company?" Mrs. Claudian shook her head. The thick dark hair shot generously with gray swung back and forth in its braid, but all he could concentrate on was one bristle whisker on her chin. "You need a *woman*, Mr. Ridley. Marry a good Italian girl and make babies. Have something to live for."

Dear God. I cannot imagine having a wife. "I rather thought I *am* living." Merely to annoy her, Hudson lifted his brandy bottle in a silent salute. "What more can a man want than spirits, sunshine, a congenial cat, and being in the center of an ancient city?"

Mrs. Claudian rolled *her* eyes so hard the whites were visible. Only an Italian mother used to bossing people could convey such sentiment. "A warm body next to him in a bed."

"While I do appreciate a willing woman, they are not worth the trouble." He'd had his fill of those sorts—for there had been many pleasant liaisons since he'd arrived in Rome—but he wasn't of a mind for a wife or the responsibilities. Especially when women wishing for marriage couldn't stomach his looks as a whole. Obviously, the requirements for a husband were very different than a casual toss in the sheets. Where he had previously been good enough to pleasure them, having him in their lives on a permanent basis suddenly made them look the other way.

And may all those women rot in hell for their prejudices.

The landlady snorted. "Whores are not the same as women bent on marriage, Mr. Ridley." A fair amount of censure threaded through the statement.

"I have learned that lesson all too well, Mrs. Claudian."

"Ha!" She shook her head. "You lie." Then she raised a thick eyebrow. "A man needs more than sex. He needs offspring to carry his name."

"Bah!" Hudson took refuge in the brandy. "Who would want my name? A failed inspector from Bow Street." A man who couldn't solve the most important case of his life. A man who'd let a killer snuff out five innocent lives.

"Not your fault." The noise she made sounded suspiciously like an oath... or she was cursing someone. He didn't have the courage to ask. "A man also needs someone to share his life and tell him he wastes his with drink and thinking." She slapped at his knee in an effort to

24

make him move from his lounging position. Then she forcefully removed the brandy bottle from his hand. "This," she held it up, "will kill you. Pickle your liver. Make you fat." Then, with another curse, she chucked it off the balcony. Seconds later, the tinkling of glass met his ears. "You are better than that, Mr. Ridley."

If looks could turn people to stone, Luna would have rendered his landlady a statue in that moment. She didn't like it when female people came too close to him, even Mrs. Claudian, who gave her scraps of fish each Sunday and bits of ham and sausage every other.

"I wonder, though," he said softly. "This is all that I am, all that I have left."

"No more of such talk."

The corners of his mouth tugged with the beginnings of a grin, for this was an argument they often indulged in. "Why? Do you wish to marry me, Mrs. Claudian?" Though he knew she was a widow, he had no idea what sort of a woman she was, other than she was at least fifteen years his senior and one hell of a force to be reckoned with.

"Of course not." Again, she smacked at his shoulder. "Men are idiots, but some have their uses." She wagged her forefinger at him. "Like you."

"How?"

"Come." The landlady led the way into the drawing room. "Clean yourself up."

"Why?" Intrigued but not overly so, Hudson heaved himself off the chair and followed her into the room.

"I have found you a client. A lady with a missing husband."

Dear God. Save me from meddling people. Slowly, he shook his head. "I have retired from that sort of work, and well you know it."

She snorted. "You need purpose again."

"Perhaps, but being a detective is not it." He couldn't take the pressure, couldn't bear to disappoint any more people by telling them he'd not solved their case.

"Neither is drinking yourself into a stupor every day." Mrs. Claudian crossed her arms at her chest. She returned his glare, then finally unbent to tap a forefinger against her temple. "You must keep your skills sharp."

"Mrs. Claudian." It was long past time to take command of this situation and any other his landlady thought to put him into. After slipping a hand around her upper arm, he gently but firmly shuttled her across the floor toward the door. "While I appreciate your interest in my life as well as reviving my career, I must reiterate that I have no compulsion to return to that sort of work." With his free hand, Hudson opened the door. "I am certain there are other highly competent men with the local polizia this woman can turn to for locating her missing husband, who, quite frankly is probably off drinking with his friends and merely needed a moment of blessed quiet away from his family."

He had seen enough loud, boisterous families in Rome during his stay to know that would give any man a headache. As for the local police force? Well, from all he'd seen, they were a collection of nodcocks who couldn't organize a proper case if their lives depended upon it. If there was truly a missing person, he prayed the family member would make other arrangements.

Which didn't include him.

"You are a coward, Mr. Ridley." Mrs. Claudian frowned at him from the doorway as he unceremoniously encouraged her into the corridor. "Why do you not wish to vanquish your demons?"

For a moment, his resolve nearly broke as he hovered on the verge of shattering beneath the emotions he never allowed anyone to see. "Sometimes it is easier to live with the demons than to court new ones," he finally said in a low voice. Then he shoved down the feelings, stuffed them down so deep within himself it would take a miracle to dig them out. "Now, if you will excuse me? I have things to do."

"What things? You are a drunk, Mr. Ridley, who needs something that will help you find your way again."

"I rather think there is no chance of that occurring." He grabbed hold of the doorknob. "Sometimes, a man reaches the end of his path and that is that." The grin he offered felt all too forced and quite false. "There are worse things, yes?" Worse things than a man who was naught but a failure. "Let me be forgotten, Mrs. Claudian. Let me vanish into obscurity."

For long moments, the older woman stared at him with narrowed eyes. "A man of your stature and reputation will never be forgotten. What should I tell Mrs. Amanti?"

He shrugged, for truly he didn't care. "Wish her good fortune and then go have your tea." Then he closed the door on his landlady and this time he made sure to throw the lock even though he suspected she had another key.

"You can't hide from your destiny, Mr. Ridley!" she hollered from the other side of the wooden panel. "God sees you and knows what you need to heal. Remember that!"

Bloody hell. Women!

"You and I have vastly differing views on that subject. Have a good evening!" Then he returned to his chair on the balcony and met the curious eyes of his cat. "Tell me, Luna, what have I done to make that crazy lady think I'm willing to go back into my previous life?"

With a meow, the cat bounced into his lap, and with an overly loud purr, she laid her front paws on his chest and began to lick his chin.

The obvious caring from the feline warmed his heart and worked to remove the bad taste left by Mrs. Claudian's meddling. "Thank you for the support." He stroked a large hand down the cat's back and then scratched her beneath the chin where she especially liked. The bright sunlight on the back of his left hand only served to bring the scar there into sharp relief. It matched the one on his cheek, given to him by that same criminal assailant. His body would never be fully healed from those injuries, and as each day passed, he remained convinced his soul wouldn't be either.

The day he walked away from Bow Street and London, he'd made his peace with whatever his future held. It was not his concern what everyone else around him wished for him to do with that life, for he would never go back.

Chapter Three

May 8, 1818
Minerva Villa
Rome

Theodosia yawned with exhaustion. Worry and fear shot through her body, for the sun had set and Jacob still hadn't returned home. Knowing her son wasn't in his own, safe bed, that he was somewhere wandering the streets of Rome had haunted her every footstep. She had turned the villa upside down in the search for him, had employed the whole of the staff into helping with the hunt, but no one could locate the boy.

Now, it didn't matter how late in the evening it had grown; she had taken herself off to gain an audience with the local constable and hope the polizia would prove helpful. Her brother had remained insistent that he ready himself for the society event he was hosting this evening. Frankly, she'd forgotten about that, couldn't begin to contemplate cooling her heels at a dinner party while Jacob could be in peril. Why her brother couldn't understand the same was beyond her, and for that she doubted she could ever forgive him. How could he think that making merry or fostering relationships between England and the well-to-do people in the Mediterranean region were more important than the fact his nephew had gone missing?

It didn't matter. Nothing did except finding her son.

She pushed open the door to her brother's small carriage the moment it rolled to a halt in front of an unimposing building that supposedly housed the constable's office. With a frown, she glanced at her driver. The dour Englishman had come to Rome with a bevy of other servants her brother had taken with him, and in this desolate place, she was glad for a countryman. "Are you quite certain this is the place?" It was at the end of a rather shabby, dark street and there was nothing to recommend it.

"I was assured by the stable master and the butler this is where one can find the nearest constable." The driver shrugged. "If you require, I can accompany you inside."

A prickle of alarm went over her skin. "I would like that very much. Thank you." It had been stupid to go haring off into the city after sunset without some sort of an escort, but her thoughts had been consumed by her missing son.

"Very good, my lady." He threw the brake on the carriage, and then while crooning to the dappled gray horse, he came down from his perch. Once he'd tied the reins to a nearby post, he turned to her. "We'd best get on with it, my lady. Night is night no matter the place, and me mum always said nothing good happened after dark."

"You are no doubt correct." She fought off the urge to shiver as they approached the nondescript door. At least there were golden squares of light, for a few of the windows of the building were illuminated. "I hope the constable is within."

"Only one way to find out, my lady."

While she appreciated the obvious being stated by her driver, Theodosia narrowed her eyes as she rapped upon the door. Seconds later, the panel swung opened, and a man dressed in evening clothes peered at her with a frown.

"Yes?"

No greeting or anything else that might set her mind at ease. Swallowing around the ball of fear and tears in her throat, she nodded. "I am Lady Ballantyne, Ambassador Wetherington's sister, and I am here to implore you to help me." Her hands shook, so she hid them in the folds of her skirting. "My son has gone missing. Earlier this afternoon, in fact. None of the men in your employ I could find on the nearby streets would take notice of me."

"I see." Those two words, spoken in heavily accented English, managed to convey a bit of contempt and even annoyance.

"Are you the local constable?"

"More or less. I am Inspector Evandar." The tall, thin man made a show of removing his pocket watch and glancing at it. "My apologies, Lady Ballantyne, but I do have an appointment."

Panic barreled into her chest. "My son is only eight years old. And he is alone."

A snort issued from the man. "Boys in Rome are rarely alone. Was he with friends before he'd gone missing?"

"Well, yes. They were playing in the courtyard of the ambassador's villa, but—"

"—then he is probably still with them. You know how time passes when boys are at play." The inspector glanced over her shoulder at her driver. "Take the woman home before she grows hysterical."

This was outside of enough! In some pique, Theodosia stamped a foot. "Of course I will become hysterical! My son is missing. I have searched the house and the grounds. He is not there. And before you ask, I questioned the boys he'd been playing with. One of them admitted he had been taken." She glared at the inspector. "What do you have to say now?"

The inspector let loose a long-suffering sigh as he replaced his pocket watch. Shooing them both out of the way, he closed the door behind him and then turned to address her again. "If you say the boy has been missing since this afternoon, that is not enough time for the *polizia* to get involved." The heavy Roman accent had her brain racing to keep up with his speech. "Come back tomorrow afternoon. Perhaps we can assist you then."

"But—"

"Where is the boy's father?"

The panic continued to well in her chest, but now it was accompanied by creeping blackness on the edges of her vision, but she stiffened her spine. *I will not faint in front of this man!* It was something of a character flaw with her. Every time she was under high duress or severe fright, her body shut down and caused a faint. Whether it was caused by the same malady of the lungs she suffered while in damp climes such as England, she couldn't say.

"Jacob's father is dead. Three years now." Though there was a slight ache in her heart to remember her husband, this man didn't need to know anything else.

Not even the truth or why she and the viscount had done what they did so long ago.

"Bah. Yet you have come here alone?" Censure was thick in his voice. Again, he darted a glance to her driver. "I rather doubt you are her protector."

As Theodosia bristled, the driver cleared his throat. "I am the carriage driver."

"Ah. Then not capable of handling a distraught lady."

"You won't take pity on her, then?"

The inspector's upper lip curled with obvious derision. "If I—or the men I work with—took pity on every story of woe that presented itself at our desks, we would never have any rest." He waved a gloved hand in obvious dismissal. "No doubt he has been distracted by something exciting and lost track of time. He will return when he is hungry. Best of luck, my lady, but I will say the streets of Rome can be a dangerous place." His gaze bounced between her and the driver. "If the boy is still missing after three days, come back."

"That will be too late!"

"It is the best I can do." The inspector proceeded them to the street.

"I rather doubt that." Anger mixed with the hot panic in her chest. "It seems to me you and your men will do anything you can *not* to follow the oath you've taken." With no apparent decorum—for there wasn't any when time was of the essence—Theodosia chased after him. "How can you have such a hard heart in this matter, Inspector?"

The other man turned to regard her again. "As I said, Rome is full of missing children. Most have runaway, and some have been turned out of their homes to find work on their own." His shrug was an elegant affair. "We do not have the capacity to watch over them."

"That's terrible!" Even after living for months as she had in Rome, she didn't know about such plights. "What of missing English children, though? This is not a life they should ever fall into."

"Ha." The inspector shook his head. "You high and mighty English. Coming here and flaunting your wealth. Thinking we all should dance attendance on you." He spat. "Bah. Find a man to take care of you, Lady Ballantyne, and have him take care of your affairs." When his gaze roved up and down her person, she glared all the more. "And if the boy doesn't return, take heart. You can have other children. It will help you forget the loss of this one." Then he stepped around her, gave her a wide berth, and continued on his way down the pavement and away from the building.

"Argh!" Tears of frustration and anger beset her, and while she wished to hurl curses or vulgarities after his retreating back, none came to mind. She shook from the force of her emotions, and with nothing else to do, looked at the driver. "Take me home, John. Obviously, no assistance will be had here."

"Of course, my lady." Enough dejection lingered in his voice, that she stifled a sob as she climbed back into the carriage. There was more compassion in this driver than in a man who was paid to help its citizens.

How I despise men in positions of power.

By the time she arrived back at her brother's villa, illumination glowed from every window in the edifice. Carriages arrived up the winding drive and let dinner party guests out. The beadwork on the ladies' gowns and the jewels at their wrists and necks glittered in that light.

Theodosia entered the house but bypassed the drawing room where the butler had directed the guests to assemble before dinner. Instead, she marched directly upstairs to her brother's rooms. She burst into his private sitting room without bothering to knock. Seeing him so nonchalantly sitting in a comfortable-looking leather armchair while reading a copy of *The Times* sent infuriated heat through her being.

"I thought you should know that the local constable has refused to take up my case, has refused to offer any assistance in finding Jacob until he has been missing a few days."

Thomas calmly folded his paper. Dressed in formal attire, he was quite handsome, and with his inherent charm, no doubt his dinner party would be a rousing success. "I am sorry to hear that."

"That is all you have to say?" She curled her hands into fists. "Jacob is missing, Thomas! He could be lost, hungry, frightened... or worse." Not even her brother knew the truth about the boy's history. Her husband had thought it best that they two—plus Doris the maid—be the only ones with that knowledge.

"What would you have me do?" He rose from the chair, and after tossing the paper onto it, he met her gaze. "I have an engagement due to begin momentarily. One I had hoped you would be at my side for." When a frown pulled his lips downward, she crossed her arms at her chest. "No matter. I can see you are upset, and that would sour the guests."

"Oh, you... you... jackanapes!" Theodosia flung her arms wide in frustration. "Why is it that no one in this city cares about my missing son except me and the servants?"

"It isn't that we don't care; it is more of a problem of not knowing how to help." When he reached out to touch her arm, she shied away. "There is every possibility Jacob will come back tonight. Boys are different creatures than girls."

She scrubbed at the tears that had fallen to her cheeks. "This dinner party means more to you than searching the streets for your own nephew?"

Guilt was evident in his expression. "This has been planned for months. Already, the guests are arriving. I cannot turn them away at this late date." He closed the distance, and this time when he slipped an arm about her shoulders, she didn't pull away, but she didn't relax into his hold. "Why don't you go lie down? You seem ready to drop from exhaustion, for you have done all that you can. Perhaps it is in fate's hands now."

"I hope you have a *lovely* time at your dinner party," she said with enough frost in her voice to ice over all of Rome. "Heaven forbid you shove everything out of the way and help me to find my son."

"Come now, Theodosia, don't be like that. Everything will turn out right as rain."

How could he know that? Pain tightened her chest, for she was nearly beside herself with worry. "I am going out to do another search."

"Take a footman. The streets of Rome are dangerous for an unaccompanied woman."

"What about for a child alone?" Emotions beset her until she was a crying, shaking mess. "As long as you have diplomacy, I'm quite certain you will find fulfillment in life." Then she swept out of the room and made sure to slam the door behind her.

Thirty minutes later saw her once more in the carriage. This time, she'd changed into the beautiful navy silk gown she'd intended to wear for the dinner party, mostly because it was readily available—Doris had draped it across the bed in readiness for tonight before the chaos ensued—and the hem of the other dress was dirty with the muck of the city streets from when she'd gone out earlier.

The kind housekeeper had heard of her plight and frustration. She'd pulled Theodosia aside and told her about a man who lived not far from the villa who used to work for Bow Street in London. Apparently, he had a knack for finding lost people and things, but he was a bit of a grumpy man with enough prickles to keep everyone away.

It was a risk she had to take, for he was her only choice at this point. Out of spite and the wish to be left alone, Theodosia had not taken a footman with her or even a maid. She was a widow, drat it, and a mother nearly hysterical because her only child was missing. No man in his right mind would seek to molest her.

"Here we are, my lady." The driver opened the carriage door and assisted her out. "Would you like me to come with you?"

"No, thank you John. This is something I should take care of myself, but I shall scream if I need help." She stared up at the rather imposing boarding house with ivy spreading out over most of the front brickwork. In the faint illumination from a couple of lamps on the street, it gave off an interesting air, and there were no vagrants lurking about. It couldn't be all bad. Especially since the property seemed well kept. "Let us hope I have better fortune here than with the constable."

"No matter what, my lady, we *will* find the young viscount."

"I appreciate that comfort." She held those humble words to her heart as she approached the green-painted door. As she pulled a crumpled scrap of paper from her reticule, she nodded. "I shall need number eight." Knots of anxiety tugged through her gut, but Theodosia straightened her spine, yanked open the front door, and marched along the narrow corridor toward a set of equally narrow, wooden stairs. Her footsteps echoed in the small space. Savory scents of dinner wafted to her nose, and though her stomach growled in hunger, there was no time to stop and beg for a repast.

On the second level, another narrow, dimly lit corridor presented itself. Behind the doors she passed, the low buzz of conversation or laughter drifted to her ears. Perhaps under different circumstances, she might have wondered at the lives of the people who lived in this building, but for now, all of her attention lay focused upon finding the apartment she sought.

At the end of the hall was number eight. Without preamble, she tucked the scrap of paper away and then rapped smartly on the door. This was as daring as she'd even been, for while she'd been married, her husband had taken the reins of any sort of messy matter or situation. *I so miss you, Nathaniel.* When the door was yanked abruptly open, she gasped, for the large man regarding her with narrowed eyes was quite unexpected.

"What the devil do you want? I have told Mrs. Claudian numerous times that I am retired."

Theodosia's eyebrows went up. "I... I don't know who that is."

"Oh?" Some of the annoyance went out of his expression. "Good." Then he stood aside. "Come." He gestured her inside. "The parlor's not much, and don't expect tea. The landlady is off duty once dinnertime is over, and I'm fumble fingers enough over my own stove."

Those words were a jumble in her mind as she entered the apartment and was shown into a small room to the left of the front door. She had a glimpse of another, larger room off to the right, and a flash of white that might have been a cat, then they both went out of her line of vision. The parlor was well-appointed if a tiny bit shabby and dated, but it wasn't lavish or ostentatious. And neither was it a mess as one would expect of bachelor rooms.

Assuming her unwilling host was that.

"What do you want?" At least he went straight to the point. To say nothing of the fact his baritone was both pleasing and arresting. "It is highly irregular for you to be here in any capacity as a genteel lady with morals."

"I am a widow, Inspector Ridley, and am afforded a certain freedom of perambulation." Really, his attitude bordered on rudeness, and she was quite done with *that* for this evening.

"How do you know my name?" Wariness showed in his expression. "And I haven't been an inspector for years."

"My brother's housekeeper told me of you." Perhaps it had been folly to come alone after all. Fissions of alarm played her spine, but she couldn't tear her attention away from him.

The whole of Theodosia's attention centered on the man who stood in the center of the space; with his lack of manners, he'd not even offered her a chair.

Not classically or even accidentally attractive by any stretch, Mr. Ridley was a large man. Tall, nearly six feet, with a barrel chest and strong arms that were crossed at that chest as he frowned, watching her as if she were naught but an annoying fly. That powerful build would go to fat in a few years. She sniffed and then nodded. Yes, there it was. The scent of brandy. If he continued on that destructive path of chasing the bottom of a brandy bottle or indulging in rich foods, he would definitely lose the form he enjoyed now.

"That isn't a good enough explanation," he groused. True to the rumors, he was a grump.

Not that it mattered, for Theodosia wasn't quite finished with her perusal of his person. He had a commanding presence about him; in fact, his presence filled the room—the whole of the apartment—but it was the way he studied her with intense, ice-blue eyes that momentarily robbed her of breath. For whatever reason, she didn't wish to be found lacking by this man, who she suspected didn't miss even a tiny detail.

In the faint illumination from candle-lit sconces on the wall, his messy black hair held glimmers of gray, for he wasn't a young man. That was appealing in and of itself, but he *was* English, and there was a hint of aristocratic blood in the shape of his nose, which was slightly crooked as if he had seen his fair share of fights in the past, as well as with the set of his rugged jaw. Her gaze flicked to an angry, jagged scar that marred his left cheek and continued on across his temple, and though she wished to know the story of how he'd acquired that, she remained silent on the subject while they stared each other down.

"Oh, bother. This is wasting time," she said, and rooted in her reticule for a calling card. Finally finding one, she offered it to him, resisting the urge to gasp when he snatched it from her fingers. "My son has gone missing. I am told you are the best at finding people, so I would like to engage your services."

He snorted with apparent derision as he glanced at her card. "I am retired from such work."

Was every man in Rome frustrating? There was no shame in pouring out her story. "You are my last hope, Mr. Ridley. I have searched everywhere for my son. He has vanished. One of the boys he had been playing with said he'd been snatched and taken. That leaves me with no options and a sick feeling in the pit of my belly."

As a new wash of tears sprang into her eyes, she accepted the lawn handkerchief he handed her. Not crisply new, it had been freshly laundered, and as she dabbed her eyes with it, the faint scents of cedarwood and orange reached her nose.

"I *am* sorry, Lady Ballantyne." The annoyance in his voice had modulated slightly, and those hints of empathy beckoned to her. "As I said, I am retired. There is reason for that. Besides, child abduction is sticky business and out of my purview. Perhaps the polizia can help."

At the last second, Theodosia stifled a sob. "I have already asked the local constable shortly before coming here." She shook her head. "He did not take my plea seriously and said to come back in three days if Jacob is still missing."

"Well, he isn't wrong in part of that. Sometimes boys just lose track of time." After he pocketed the calling card, he edged her toward the door. "Perhaps you merely need to sleep. Rest will put perspective on the high emotion you currently labor under."

"Grr!" She didn't apologize for the growl. "I am quite sick of pompous men thinking I am hysterical and upset for no reason."

His eyes widened and she saw flecks of deeper blue in those lighter irises. "Oh, I am quite certain you have a reason. I have seen far too many mothers who have lost children over the course of my career to discount your emotion."

"Then why won't you listen to me? Help me?" She shook her head, suddenly frantic, when he guided her to the front door of the apartment. "I had hoped you would be different, Mr. Ridley, since Bow Street men carry an impressive reputation."

"I am neither with that organization nor are we in London, my lady." He wrenched open the door. "And we all must face disappointment sooner or later." A muscle ticced in his cheek, and again she wondered over how he'd come by that scar. "Besides, I left Bow Street much in disgrace, so I am certain I'm not the proper man for this job."

"I don't care about your reputation, but I do care about my son." Desperate and in need of answers, she clutched at his arm. "Please do this for me, Mr. Ridley. I will pay you handsomely." Her swallow was audible before she came to an odd sense of clarity about him. "Perhaps in this way you can find a bit of redemption for yourself." When he remained silent, but confliction raged across his face, she relaxed, but only slightly. "Please call at the address on that card tomorrow morning. We shall discuss further plans then."

A soft round of cursing sailed through the air behind her. "I haven't agreed to take this case."

Theodosia allowed a barely there grin as she glanced over her shoulder at him. "No, but you will. Until tomorrow, Inspector."

Would her gambit pay off? Only time would tell, but now she felt hope, where she hadn't before.

Chapter Four

May 9, 1818
Mrs. Claudian's boarding house
Rome

At half past ten the next morning, Hudson frowned at Luna as he tied his cravat into a simple knot and arranged the folds to his liking. "What?"

The cat meowed. She licked the tip of her left front paw.

"You think involving myself in a case is a bad idea." It wasn't a question.

His feline companion merely blinked and stared.

"And an equally bad idea to call upon Lady Ballantyne." He snagged her calling card from the edge of his wash basin. Flowers had been sketched into two corners of the stock, and her name was done in a scroll. When he lifted it to his nose, the faint scent of lilacs teased his nose. It reminded him of the few times he'd been in the English countryside in the summer and those bushes were prolific, their perfume on the breeze. "She is a viscountess who moves in circles beyond mine," he told the cat.

Who wasn't apparently impressed. Luna curled her tail around her four paws and watched him with an impassive expression.

"A widow, at that," Hudson amended, and didn't know why he felt that he should add a rejoinder to the previous statement. To say nothing of those silver-blue eyes with the darker gray ring around the irises. Never had he seen such beautiful eyes. They had been shooting daggers at him last night, of course, but they were still haunting. "I imagine she's quite frantic to find her son." Yet he'd more or less kicked her out of his rooms last night, after abjectly refusing to help her. It had been the height of bad manners, but he *had* told her twice he was retired.

Yet, the emotion she'd exhibited, the tears she'd shed in his presence, hadn't been for show or pretend. She had truly been distraught.

Luna hopped from the side of the wash basin to the ledge of the small window at his other side. She glanced outside and then back to him with a meow that sounded suspiciously like a question.

"Yes, of course I feel badly that her son is missing. I'm not a monster," he told the cat while peering at his reflection in the cloudy, oval-shaped mirror hanging on the wall over the washstand. "However, Rome is not London. I am out of my element. Don't have my usual resources."

His cat licked one corner of her mouth.

"Fine."

Obviously, the cat didn't care that he was using such a thing as an excuse. Finished with his toilet, Hudson moved to the foot of the bed where he'd left his second-best jacket. Made of sapphire superfine, it had been a gift from a former client after he'd managed to locate the man's wife. She'd fallen, hit her head, and then suffered from temporary amnesia and couldn't find her way home. The man had been so grateful at the conclusion of that case that he'd sent Hudson straightaway to his own tailor for a new set of clothing. Hudson, being the humble person he was, had managed to talk the client out of a wardrobe and instead had settled for a waistcoat and that jacket.

"I shall go see what the widow has to say. Will that make you happy?" After struggling into the jacket, he did up the buttons and then tugged on the hem of his plain tan waistcoat, smoothed his palms along the sides of his hips encased in buff-colored breeches. "No doubt by the time I arrive, it will be to discover her boy has come home on his own after getting lost in a strange neighborhood while playing with his mates."

Except, she had told Hudson her son had been snatched…

Without any more excuses, he retrieved her calling card, jammed his top hat on his head, and then left the boarding house.

Minerva Villa
Rome

Hudson paced the length of the luxurious drawing room he'd been settled in upon arriving at the ambassador's residence. Lady Ballantyne might be a viscountess, but her brother was the English ambassador to Rome, and here on the Continent, that carried more weight than an English title. Though the villa had been set aside for whomever held the ambassador's post, it was decorated with gilt frames on the walls and gilded chair legs. Rich Aubusson carpeting muffled his footfalls, while the shades of green throughout the rooms in the upholstery, curtains, and carpeting put him in mind of an English spring day.

The view outside was breathtaking, with mountains in the far distance and greenery everywhere his eyes turned. A courtyard was inviting, and the scent of flowers danced on the breeze that came in through the opened windows. At this time of the year in London, the world would be drenched with rain and fog and damp.

Somehow, he had been exceptionally fortunate to land here.

He detected the aroma of lilacs in the air before the viscountess spoke. Slowly, he turned, and despite his best efforts to remain aloof, Hudson's breath stalled in his lungs. Bloody hell but the woman knew how to dress to advantage.

The gown of vibrant pink silk draped her body like a lover's caress. Though the dress itself was devoid of all ornamentation, there was one simple flounce at the hem that gave the frock a whimsical feel that belied the circumstances. A rounded bodice trimmed with white tulle and lace kept her modest breasts nestled within the fabric and put just a hint of those charms on display that kept his attention.

"Uh, Lady Ballantyne. Good morning." What the devil was wrong with him? He couldn't stop staring at the woman. Though she lived in Rome, her skin remained as pale as alabaster. What would she look like with sun-bronzed color on those arms or shoulders or cheekbones?

"I almost thought you wouldn't keep our meeting today." Her gaze darted to a carriage-style clock on the mantle. When she returned her regard to him, a hint of a blush stained her cheeks, but there was a trace of panicked fear in her eyes. "Ten more minutes and it won't be morning."

"Yes, well, that couldn't be helped." Subtle heat rose up the back of his neck, for he refused to admit that he'd been talking to his cat about just that. "Truth be told, I debated on whether I should come or not."

Her pink lips formed a frown that would have a lesser man scrambling to say something cheerful or charming merely to see her smile again. He wasn't in the business of either. "That is your prerogative, of course, but if you truly are the best in the retrieval game, why would I waste time in hiring someone else?"

Well, damn. Where he assumed flattery would have no effect on him, here he was fighting the urge to do her bidding. *Get hold of yourself, Hudson.* "Was, my lady."

"I beg your pardon?" Those melodious tones held a touch of confusion.

"I *was* the best. Those days are long past."

"Only because you are denying to yourself what is the truth." She waved him over to a grouping of furniture, and when she perched on the edge of a low settee, he dropped into a delicate chair that he hoped didn't collapse beneath his weight. "Regardless of why you are denying your skills, can you find my son, Mr. Ridley?"

Bloody hell. She was quite adamant. "Yes. I can find him, and yes, I *am* the best at what I do." He had been, at least when it had been his business to do so, but he couldn't imagine those skills had been lost over the intervening two years. "However, we need to discuss the terms of payment first." He might have a knack for the retrieval game, yet a man needed to make a living. The fact he'd retired from this sort of thing lurked in the back of his mind, for if he failed on this case, it would no doubt break this woman. That knowledge wore on a person, broke them down from the inside after seeing what human beings were capable of doing to each other.

After witnessing the very real heartbreak from friends and loved ones of the missing — and subsequently deceased — person.

I don't know if I can do this again.

"Very well." Lady Ballantyne nodded as if she'd expected that announcement. "I am prepared to give you two hundred pounds now and two hundred pounds upon the safe return of my son." One of her finely feathered blonde eyebrows raised. "Is that to your liking?"

"That is more than generous." Hell, that sort of coin would allow him to pay the rent on his rooms for an entire year and have much left over.

"Good. Do you require this agreement in writing?" The fact that she was wringing her hands was a good indication she was under high duress.

"No. I trust you." Did he, though? He who had a difficult time extending that to anyone?

"That is good to know." Slowly, she rose to her feet, as slim and graceful as any number of statues he'd seen throughout Rome, which meant Hudson had to scramble into a standing position. "Let me go quickly to fetch your retainer."

Heat crept up the back of his neck, then annoyance for wanting to make a living went through his chest. "You needn't do such a thing now."

"I do." Before he could say anything else, she'd left the room, trailing the lingering scent of lilacs behind her.

It was Hudson's turn to frown. Perhaps it was folly to even agree to take the case. He knew next to nothing about this woman or the family dynamics at play, but then, he'd solved other cases on much less. Despite his misgivings, excitement buzzed at the base of his spine. Retirement had its benefits, of course, but finding purpose for his life again would do more than wiling away the hours on his balcony.

Before he could become too lost in his thoughts, the viscountess returned with a small leather pouch clutched in one hand. "Here you are, Mr. Ridley." As soon as she crossed the carpeting, she offered the purse to him. "The agreed upon two hundred pounds."

"Thank you." He tucked the payment into his waistcoat pocket. Once she'd resumed her seat, he sank onto his recently vacated chair. "However, there is something I must make certain you are aware of before we begin."

"Yes?" Her eyelids fluttered briefly, and she leaned slightly backward as if steeling herself for a blow or bad news. Was she even aware she did so? What exactly had happened in her life to make her fear such action?

"I cannot guarantee I will find him alive." Truly, there was no way to soften those words. She needed to know that going in. Far too many eventualities ended with grief, and the earlier a person could prepare themselves, the better. "Since you haven't yet received any sort of note demanding a ransom or other instructions, there is every possibility your son was taken for a different reason altogether." He softly cleared his throat. "Every hour we delay in making progress means he might be closer to death."

"Oh." Tears welled in her unique eyes, magnifying the color, and rendering them luminous. Yet, the longer he peered into those gray depths, the more secrets he suspected she kept. Were they pertinent to his case? And if so, why did she persist in keeping them? "Why would anyone wish to kidnap my son?"

"That is one of the answers we must seek, and why I am here currently. Is there anything special about him that someone might wish to have?"

Something flickered in her eyes before she lowered her lashes and stared at her hands in her lap. Had she not told him the full truth? "Of course, I think Jacob is special. He is my son, my much-wished-for child."

Interesting. "I don't mean to be indelicate, but is he your only child?"

"Yes. There were some... difficulties conceiving." She brushed at the moisture on one cheek, but it was the quivering chin — that damned pointed, pixyish chin in her oval face — that caught and held his attention. The blush staining her pale cheeks had the power to fascinate him, but he wouldn't let it.

"I am sorry to hear that." No wonder she was so distraught.

"Thank you. It was rather devastating to both me and Lord Ballantyne."

"I can imagine it was." This was territory in which he had no experience in which to speak. To want children but never have them. It was a secret dream of his to have a family of his own, but with the state of the world as it was, he couldn't in good conscience actively pursue that. "Pray, continue. Tell me about the viscount."

The slight incline of her chin denoted the fact she was probably quite stubborn if given the chance. "My husband died three years ago, but though Jacob is the next Viscount Ballantyne, he is too young to take up his seat in the House of Lords. Regarding finances, my husband wasn't a wealthy man. The title didn't come with much coin or property, but the name carries much respect. He was quite proud of that."

"So then there is no funding for a ransom." Interesting.

"Indeed." She looked at him and tears glittered in her eyes. "Nathanial had no political enemies I am aware of. In fact, he did his level best to avoid such discussions. Neither did men within the *ton* hate him. He was nothing but proper and quite congenial. A true gentleman who treated everyone equally."

"I see. A fair-minded man, though, could have made enemies all the same. There are some in England who don't wish for progress or change." Hudson kept his own counsel on that. Just because a man was presumably well-liked didn't mean that he was. It also didn't mean he hadn't held secrets. Though a wave of protection inexplicably rose for this woman, he tamped those feelings. His clients were always upset; that was understandable, but the moment he considered them in a personal light? Made a connection that went beyond employer/employee? It made him vulnerable and that meant he could make mistakes.

Never again.

"Would being one down for votes in the House of Lords be reason for someone to kidnap my child?" She sounded properly horrified.

"Human nature is oftentimes an ugly thing, my lady." Hudson shrugged. "However, perhaps the kidnapping has nothing at all to do with your deceased husband. And, as you say, Jacob is too young to take up the vote." Had she loved the man? How long had their union lasted? How had he died? Questions went around in his mind like ponies on a loop, but there would be time enough for all of that.

Lady Ballantyne frowned. Hudson doubted she was accustomed to this sort of scrutiny or trauma, but there was nothing for it. "Then *why* was Jacob taken?"

Why indeed. It was still too early in the investigation for him to answer with any sort of certainty. "What is *your* lineage, Lady Ballantyne?" As he waited for her answer, he removed a small, worn, leatherbound notebook from the interior pocket of his jacket and the nub of a pencil. It was essential to take notes to refer back on later.

"The usual bloodlines, I suppose. Nothing special and certainly not close enough to royalty to make a difference." She pressed her lips together. Would they feel as plush as they looked if he were to steal a kiss? "My husband was a viscount; my father the same. Neither of them did anything controversial, nor did they keep company with the wrong sorts."

"Ah." Hudson scribbled a line or two in the notebook. Oh, he knew who she was, for he had made discreet inquiries after he'd sent her on her way. Desperate, plain women who were rendered beautiful in the right light didn't merely appear in his parlor without making an impression. This was Rome, much different from the streets of London, and the polizia were bumbling idiots when it came to things like this.

Or anything else that required immediate aid.

To say nothing about his natural curiosity. There was something about this woman that intrigued him over and above her plight. It was why he'd agreed to meet with her today.

"My father is dead, buried in the Derbyshire countryside on the estate he loved. My oldest brother Percy has taken up those reins."

That shouldn't make a difference.

"What of your other brother, Thomas?"

"He is enjoying his ambassadorial duties."

"I imagine that he is. There is a certain amount of freedom offered in the position." Hudson offered a trace of a grin. "What was your son doing just before he was taken?"

"The usual things he does." Her shrug was an elegant affair. God, she was a bewitching creature. "Playing with a few other boys his age in the courtyard. They live nearby. I remember seeing flashes of light off something he had in his hand... Oh no." A gasp broke the silence as she looked at him. "Prior to that, Jacob had been in my bedchamber. He enjoys playing with the contents of my jewelry cases, likes to feel the texture of each piece, see the gemstones sparkle."

Ah, now they were getting somewhere. "What color were the flashes?"

"Green. Brilliant green in the sunlight. Does that mean something?"

Hudson scribbled in his notebooks. "Perhaps not, but it *is* a clue. Did you have an emerald in your possession?"

"I don't, personally." Again, she gasped. It was becoming habit. "Nathanial did, though. He showed it to me only once, years ago, just after we'd married. He was proud of that gemstone. Forty-three carats and was rumored to have belonged to Marie Antoinette herself." In her enthusiasm, the tears faded, and her eyes sparkled as if they were gems of their own. "He always maintained he had won the emerald in a game of cards. Said in this way he'd saved it from Napoleon's own men."

"What was he saving it for?"

"Who can say? To fund our future? To give Jacob a cushion? We never spoke about it, and I didn't see the emerald again after that." Lady Ballantyne shook her head. "He must have hidden it among my jewelry. We rarely entertained, so those caskets were seldom opened. Jacob must have come upon it, thought it was a toy for its size... Oh God." She swayed a bit on the settee, and for a brief moment, he thought she might faint, but then she got hold of herself and straightened her spine.

"Indeed." Hudson jotted down a few more notes. "Perhaps we have arrived at the reason your son was taken. Mind you, this is only a theory and might not be the cause, but it's certainly an avenue we can explore. The question now is, by whom."

Shadows flitted over her face but were gone at her next sigh. "Do you think one of the boys told someone about the emerald? Do you believe a parent is responsible?" Panic threaded through the questions. "If so, why didn't the boy simply steal the gemstone and run off with it? Why involve my son?"

"Calm yourself, my lady. It won't do to jump to conclusions." He tucked his notebook and pencil back into the pocket. "There are several explanations." Then he made the mistake of leaning over and touching her hand. A heated jolt jumped up his arm to his elbow.

Her eyes rounded. "Are there?"

"Of course."

"Will you tell me?"

"Not right now. It is not my habit of revealing too much prematurely." Then he stood. "However, there are many things on the list which need investigating."

"Such as?"

"We are going to talk with the boy who told you Jacob had been taken." Perhaps the child had other details he hadn't divulged.

"We?" How the viscountess managed to infuse that one-word inquiry with such curiosity, he would never know, but she rose and some of the sadness in her expression faded. "You mean to include me in your case?"

Her surprise was refreshing. Most of the time, his clients refused to dirty their hands. "Of course. I didn't figure you would wish to leave anything to chance. You seem quite interested in finding Jacob for yourself."

"What a lovely surprise. Thank you." The tentative smile she offered heated his insides.

Tamping on the reaction, Hudson nodded. "That is if you don't mind being seen in the company of a wreck of a man like me." His scars weren't easily forgotten.

She tsked her tongue, and immediately her gaze went to the left side of his face. "You are distinguished, Mr. Ridley, not disfigured. Remember that."

For a few seconds, he was rendered speechless. After clearing his throat, he nodded. "Besides, you will know where the boy resides." Feeling lighter than he had in many months, he winked and then quickly chastised himself mentally. "If you have nothing else to do, my lady?"

"I do not just now."

Oh, she would be trouble, but then, he refused to let that happen. They had a business relationship only. He did *not* need an entanglement like her in his life.

Chapter Five

Uncommonly thrilled that the man she'd hired thought enough of her to include her in his investigation, Theodosia excused herself from the drawing room in order to procure a bonnet and gloves. When she came back down, she met her brother in the corridor a few feet from the drawing room.

"Ah. Have you popped in to say hello to Mr. Ridley?"

"No. I was actually searching for you." Thomas frowned. "Why is Mr. Ridley here?"

She tugged on her gloves. "I engaged his services. To find Jacob."

"Ah." Guilt and sorrow mixed in her brother's expression. "I apologize, Theodosia. I should have taken your fears seriously when it happened."

"You should have, but there is no need to concern yourself now." She briefly laid her fingers on his arm. "Mr. Ridley seems to be quite capable." Of course, Theodosia didn't tell

Thomas of the inappropriate attraction that had snapped between them, an invisible current, that pull which she couldn't ignore. For now, she would. They couldn't afford a distraction — or a disaster. Though she hadn't been in the former Bow Street Man's company for long, she already felt relieved knowing he was in charge of the case, but there were times she could hardly breathe because Jacob was still missing without a trace or even a word. "He *will* solve this."

"What now? A night has passed and its midday of today." A hard look crossed Thomas' face. "Seems to me that man hasn't performed any miracles."

"I just hired him." Annoyance stabbed through her chest. "He is hunting for clues, has just concluded an interview with me." She gestured a hand back toward the drawing room door. "You can talk to him yourself if you wish."

"I do not." He peered into her face. "Did you not have a maid with you during that interview?"

"Of course not." Why did he insist on treating her as a young woman, still innocent? "I am a widow and a concerned mother. He is an investigator. Some of the topics discussed are highly personal."

"It's not proper."

She pointed her gaze to the ceiling and blew out a breath before focusing on her brother again. "There is no impropriety." Nothing scandalous would occur between them for the simple fact she wouldn't allow it. *I am not looking for a romance, and certainly not while Jacob is still missing.* "In moments, he and I will go out and canvass for information."

Thomas crossed his arms over his chest. "Well, I don't like the looks of him."

"Don't be crass." She frowned. "What's wrong with him? To my mind, he is as English and proper as you or I." In fact, that sapphire jacket had brought out the intensity in his ice blue eyes, and she could hardly ignore the strength he exuded as he'd talked with her.

"I know you aren't as coy as all that." He pulled her to the side and lowered his voice. "I made some discreet inquiries after you told me you'd called upon him last night."

Her heartbeat accelerated as annoyance once more speared through her. "And?"

"His reputation isn't exactly sterling. He is a layabout, a drunk, seems more rough and tumble than the company you should keep."

"Does any of that mean he cannot work this case?"

"I haven't been apprised of his skill."

"Then you have no right to judge him."

"Theodosia, please." A huff escaped him. "I don't trust him."

"Most likely he doesn't trust you either." Tit for tat, brother. "If I discover this case is beyond his skills, I shall withdraw my support, but I won't have you disparage him before he's gotten started." She cocked an eyebrow. "And yes, I will lend my assistance for as long as he wishes. It's not as if I am allowing him to court me."

"Perish the thought," Thomas mumbled beneath his breath. "Otherwise, you and I would need to have a serious discussion on what is expected of you."

"Argh!" She balled a hand into a fist but then forced herself to relax. "I am not a young girl anymore, Thomas, and quite frankly, I'll do what I please, when it pleases *me*." A sound from the drawing room made her tilt her head to one side, for it sounded like a soft snort but she couldn't be sure.

"Don't let your desperation pin all of your hopes on this man. He is fallible."

"Isn't that rather the best sort of person? Who wants to go around with perfection all the time? Can you imagine how tedious that would be?" She made a shooing motion with a hand and then set the bonnet onto her head. "I shall leave you to your work." Knots of worry pulled in her belly as she tied the ribbons beneath her chin. "I expect to put in long hours with Mr. Ridley today so don't assume I will take dinner with you."

A frosty laugh came from her brother. "Indeed, for we can't even assume the man is civilized enough to do that in mixed company."

"Oh, you… you… pompous arse!" In her agitation, Theodosia stamped a foot. "You will be in his debt once he finds my son. He will prevail where you didn't care to."

"Unless he only wants your coin."

She tossed her head. "Mr. Ridley is the best chance I have, Thomas." Tears sprang into her eyes. "Please don't jeopardize that by antagonizing him."

Again, his expression crumbled. "I would never…"

"I am going to break soon," she admitted in a small voice. "Mr. Ridley gives me back hope. He is good at what he does, so please have faith. I will need that support."

Thomas nodded. "Best wishes that you will find a clue today."

"Thank you." With her head held high, Theodosia continued along the corridor and then entered the drawing room, where she ran right into the hard wall that was Mr. Ridley's body. "Oomph!"

"Steady, my lady." For the space of a few heartbeats, his arms were around her as she worked to find her footing. "I would apologize for eavesdropping, but since the subject matter was me, I won't."

That deep baritone went through her and tickled the inside of her chest if that were possible. Only then did she realize how tall he was, how she had to tilt her head back in order to meet his gaze, and just how wide his shoulders were, how hard his chest felt beneath the palm she'd rested upon it. Cedarwood and orange teased her nose. "Um…" What had he been talking about? When she stepped away, he released his hold immediately. "I apologize for what my brother said."

He narrowed his gaze. "I didn't need you to defend me."

"I certainly wasn't going to let him continue on in that vein. He doesn't know you."

"Neither do you." Shadows flitted across his face, and his eyes took on a haunted look.

"I expect we shall spend much time together in the foreseeable future, so that will obviously change." Drat the man for making himself more interesting.

For long moments, he regarded her but gave nothing away regarding his thoughts. Finally, he nodded curtly. "Perhaps. Come, then. We are wasting time."

Theodosia lifted her face to the sunlight. If she could forget about the reason for the walk, the outing would have been quite lovely. Mr. Ridley had slowed his gait to accommodate her shorter stride, and as of yet, there hadn't been much conversation, but then, perhaps it wasn't needed. In some ways, she appreciated silence in a man; some of them felt compelled to blather on about nothing in particular.

"Tell me about your marriage to the viscount."

The question was startingly enough, but having his baritone cut into her thoughts made her start. She glanced at him beyond the short brim of her bonnet, but he stared ahead. "I was wed to Nathaniel for six lovely years." A grin tugged at the corners of her lips. "Though I was nineteen when we'd wed and I scarcely had experience of life, none of that mattered. We learned from each other and had the best time together."

"Were you happy?"

"Oh, very much so." Then her grin faded. "I was devastated when he died."

"Of natural causes?"

"No." A ball of tears crowded her throat and temporarily prevented her from speaking. After a few hard swallows, she continued. "It was a random robbery on the street as he walked to his carriage one night after being at his club."

"Interesting." Mr. Ridley halted their walk and turned to her. "Why did you not mention that before?"

She frowned. "I didn't think it pertinent. It was something that happened. Unfortunate, of course, but London isn't always the safest place. You especially should know that." As much as she tried to prevent it, her gaze slid to his left cheek. "Er, I mean, for what you saw while with Bow Street."

Those intense ice-blue eyes seemed to bore into her soul. A shiver of *something* went up her spine, but she couldn't immediately determine what it was. Surely it couldn't be... need. She had been without the attentions of a man in any capacity. Why would she suddenly feel that for Mr. Ridley?

"Everything is pertinent to something else, Lady Ballantyne. Those reasons remain hidden until the appropriate time." One of his dark eyebrows rose in question. "Was the crime ever solved?"

"It was not." She shook her head. "My father hired a Bow Street man to investigate, of course, but either the mugger had done his job all too well or he fled Town immediately afterward, or possibly found his own end by unrelated causes." When she shrugged, she couldn't help wondering what he might be getting at. "But as I said before, my husband didn't have enemies."

"Hmph." He tugged the small leatherbound notebook from his jacket pocket and then scribbled down a note. "Once a pattern emerges, everything becomes connected. I merely need to find more pieces to see a pattern," he said in a low voice, almost to himself.

"I'm afraid I don't understand what that means."

"Currently, my lady, you are on a need-to-know basis, and right now, there is nothing of significance to tell." After he tucked the notebook and pencil stub away, he set them into motion once more. "Why have you not married again?"

Well, that was a bit personal, but then, he *was* an investigator. "I almost vanished while in mourning; I felt Nathaniel's death that hard. Yet I had to be strong for Jacob's sake. Afterward, I was lonely. I'm not one who wishes to change the world, and I'm happiest when I have a man at my side." Was that too revealing?

"Has no one asked to court you?" Nothing except mild interest rang in those tones.

Heat seeped into her cheeks. "I haven't been willing to take up that particular challenge, but when I came to Rome to visit my brother, he has actively been introducing me to eligible men."

"That you've rebuffed, no doubt."

"I have." She chuckled. "However, right before my son went missing, I'd promised Thomas I would be receptive to meeting a few of his candidates." All levity went out of her person. Threads of darkness flirted with the edges of her vision, and she swayed. So much so that she clutched at Mr. Ridley's arm to remain upright. "But then Jacob left and now all of that seems of vain and superficial."

"You are allowed to feel hope at the same time you are under duress." He glanced at her with concern in his eyes. "It won't always be like this. Eventually, you can enjoy the normality of life again."

"Perhaps." Though she didn't deserve any such consideration, to say nothing of love. If her past actions had led to this current pass... With a shake of her head, she dashed the tears away the best she could. "This is where the boy lives." It was a long line of row houses with a beautiful courtyard in a square between buildings. Aging in spots, it wasn't a bad place to raise children.

"Ah. Good." With further comment, Mr. Ridley marched up the short walkway and proceeded to rap curtly upon the nondescript door. Once it swung open, he nodded and gave the woman standing there what he no doubt thought was a charming grin.

Theodosia couldn't tell since he wasn't facing her at the moment. She nodded at the dark-haired woman who wore an apron dusted with flour. "Hullo, Mrs. DeMarco. Is Luca at home?"

"He's out." She waved a work-reddened hand. "Somewhere."

Mr. Ridley cleared his throat. "Perhaps you can answer a few questions we have regarding your son."

"What has he done now?" Immediately, Mrs. DeMarco's expression hardened. "That boy is nothing but trouble."

"My own boy was kidnapped yesterday, and yours told me he had been snatched," Theodosia quickly explained. "I wanted to know if he could remember what the men looked like."

"He said that was a lie." The other woman shook her head. Fear jumped into her eyes. "He doesn't know where Jacob is."

"What?" Theodosia frowned. "What happened, then? Where is my son?" When she took a step toward Mrs. DeMarco, the stouter lady retreated.

"No one knows. Your boy must have run off."

"Impossible!" Annoyance speared through her chest. "Why do you deny your son's story? He told me that as soon as I noticed Jacob missing. Why would he lie?"

"I must go." The other woman pushed backward into her house, and as the door swung closed, Mr. Ridley caught the edge of it in a big hand.

"Who are you afraid of, Mrs. DeMarco? Who has made you leery of speaking about the missing boy?"

"I… Goodbye, sir. Do not come back. I don't want trouble." Then the door was firmly shut at the expense of his gloved fingertips being nipped.

"Obviously, whomever took your child has threatened the rest of his playmates as well as their parents." Again, he took out his notebook, scribbled for a few seconds, and then replaced it in his pocket. Then he glanced at Theodosia. "Highly interesting."

"Why? We learned nothing." The way the former inspector's mind worked baffled her.

"Not so. We have learned your son was indeed taken and said kidnappers don't wish for the boys of his set to talk about it. That speaks volumes." Unlike what he'd done on the way over, Mr. Ridley offered her his crooked arm. "There's nothing for it but to escort you home."

Hot panic threaded through her chest. She tamped it as best she could as she laid her fingers on his forearm. The muscles were solid beneath her fingertips, and once more, the temptation of wanting to feel that banked power around her flared. "Nothing will be gained by going home and wringing my hands."

"I think you are made of rather sterner stuff than that, Lady Ballantyne." The wry humor in the words worked to tug a small smile from her. "However, the person who threatened Mrs. DeMarco or even the other boys must wield some power in Rome. Now we must ask ourselves if the crime isn't somehow connected to your brother's position."

Knots of anxiety pulled in her belly. "I cannot imagine that it is. Thomas has friends and connections all over the city. He is very well liked and respected."

"Not everyone in every place will find favor with everyone. The world, in general, is a rather unkind and hideous place."

As they walked, and since she was on his left side, Theodosia studied his profile. A proud but humble man, a strong man used to protecting others and ferreting out the truth. The scars on his cheek and temple spoke to that passionate urge of defense. Her fingers itched to smooth the breeze-ruffled shock of dark hair from his forehead into some semblance of order, but she didn't dare. He didn't invite intimacy or even friendship, and there wasn't either in their relationship of investigator and client.

Still, what secrets did he keep? What drove this man to put his life in danger for people he didn't know well? How had he come to this pass?

And perhaps more to the point, would Jacob find him interesting once the boy was either found or returned? *What a silly notion,*

Theo, she chided herself. *If you are seeking a father for the boy, this man couldn't – shouldn't – fill that role.*

"Jacob is such a bright child, and quite curious. He always has questions, and he likes nothing more than to poke about exploring seemingly everything around him."

"It is good for a boy to be such. I have no use for children who are spoiled or pompous."

Indeed, what had been his experience with children? Did he wish for a family of his own? Merely another two questions to add to the growing list she kept in her head. "Oh, he has never been spoiled. In fact, Nathanial and I made certain he was never given anything that might make him into a brat." Every day she had been thankful they'd been able to provide a life for him; it was infinitely better than what he would have had if they hadn't intervened in fate's plan.

"You dote on him." It wasn't a question.

"Of course I do. My own childhood was loving and made me feel safe. Though my brothers often bickered with each other, they got on well with me and our parents." When she lifted her hand from his arm, he was quick to encourage her fingers to remain resting on his sleeve. "I wished to give Jacob every good thing that life offered, to teach him that privileged doesn't mean pompous and arrogant."

"I have no doubts you are an excellent mother to the child." He glanced at her, and their gazes connected. "Does he resemble you?"

Oh dear. What to say that wouldn't have those intense eyes shadowed with judgment? "Uh, I like to think he does." Didn't all mothers wish for that? It didn't matter where the child had gotten its start. "He has blond hair and the kindest hazel eyes." Though hers were blue-gray and Nathaniel's had been brown, and since they had more or less adopted the boy, of course he wouldn't take after them. "Sometimes, when he smiles, he has the look of royalty." Her chuckle sounded all too forced to her own ears. "But that is probably wishful thinking."

Had it been fortunate that no one had noticed that resemblance as of yet? That no one would wonder upon his true parentage?

Anxiety from those thoughts suddenly assailed her. Had his taking been a grand plot all along and now he was paying the price for the kindness she and her husband had enacted eight years before? Surely that wouldn't be the case. Not here in Rome. Not now. Too much time had passed, and no one had known what they'd done. Doris certainly wouldn't have told. Despite her and Nathaniel's careful and clever planning, had the truth somehow become known?

Oh, God.

Her breath came in too-quick pants while her chest tightened, made it difficult to draw air into her lungs. But there was no mistaking this as the sickness that used to assail her in damp, dirty London. Oh, no, this was pure panic, and if she didn't get hold of herself, everything would start to crumble. Despite wishing for calm, her symptoms grew worse. Darkness hovered around the edges of her vision, grew so bad that lightheadedness came over her. With a stumble and a missed step, Theodosia fell into the first stages of a faint.

"Lady Ballantyne, are you well?" When she didn't answer immediately and instead sagged into his side, he muttered a curse. "Forgive the familiarity." Seconds later, Mr. Ridley scooped her up into his arms as if she were naught but a wayward child.

"Oh, please stop. Put me down." The heat of embarrassment seeped into Theodosia's cheeks. Her words were breathless, and she shoved weakly against his shoulder, but he wasn't having it, and she had to restrain herself from exploring that muscled shoulder.

"You are obviously suffering from a reaction. I'll wager reality is finally sinking in. But fear not, I will have you home soon." Without another word, he continued on his way toward the ambassador's residence as if assisting helpless women was merely another service that he offered.

"Thank you for the kindness." With nothing else to do, and her head still spinning a bit, Theodosia gave herself over to his care. She rather enjoyed being taken care of, and the feel of his strong, protective arms around her worked to unravel her commonsense. Being held against that hard wall of his wide chest had the power to see her undone.

If she would let herself break all the way.

Fifteen minutes later saw them back at Minerva Villa. Immediately, the butler was concerned at her fading health, and since Thomas was somewhere else in Rome having a meeting, she directed Mr. Ridley to put her into the drawing room. "Carruthers, please order tea. I am famished and a touch parched." To her rescuer, she said in a hushed whisper, "I am not an invalid and not sick enough to warrant being tucked away in bed." Then another round of heat went through her cheeks to think of something as intimate as a bedchamber and this man in the same sentence.

You are becoming naught but a silly goose, Theo.

"This is why you should take the time and rest," Mr. Ridley said in a low voice as he gently deposited her on a sofa. Shortly after, he brought over a footstool with an embroidered brocade cushion. "If you let yourself give into the horrible thoughts or worse-case scenarios, nothing good will come of that." The touch of his fingers on her ankle sent shockwaves up her leg as he encouraged her foot onto the cushion. His gaze met hers while he did the same with her other foot. "For Jacob, you must guard your own health, hmm?"

"I am doing my best." Though she wanted nothing more than to have the permission to break apart, to sob out her fears and worries, to rail at the heavens for allowing her son to be taken in the first place, she kept as calm as she could and removed her bonnet. She tossed the headgear to a cushion of the sofa beside her then did the same with her gloves.

"That is all I can ask."

"Mmm." With a quick glance at the open door to assure her they were still alone, she caught one of his gloved hands, squeezed his fingers. "I appreciate you looking after me, Mr. Ridley." Her chin wobbled and a wash of tears filled her eyes. "I'm afraid this situation has me rather at sixes and sevens, and not being in control of any of it has put me at a disadvantage."

"Your reaction is completely justified." He searched her face with that intense gaze of his, and for whatever reason she held her breath. "But this, perhaps, is not." Then he leaned over her and kissed her. That gentle, fleeting press of his lips against hers caught her off guard and sent her senses pinwheeling. All too soon, he pulled away and put a few feet of distance between them as shock etched itself through his expression. "I apologize. That wasn't well done, and hardly professional."

"I…" She could still feel the touch of those firm but supple lips briefly cradling hers. That tiny show of affection plowed through the gates she'd kept around her feelings ever since she'd lost Nathaniel and left her almost gasping for more of his attention. "Think nothing of it, Mr. Ridley. We were both gripped by high emotion and drama."

"Be that as it may, you can be assured it will never happen again." A hard expression crossed his face; no doubt he berated himself for doing something so out of character.

Theodosia was spared answering, for Carruthers brought in a tea service on a silver tray.

"How are you feeling, my lady?" The man of indeterminate years bustled about after setting the tray upon a nearby table. He fussed with preparing a cup of tea to her specifications and then put it into her hands. "The staff wishes for an update. We know what a terrible time this must be for you."

A tear slipped to her cheek despite her resolve to banish them. "Thank you. I am better now that I'm home." Heat filled her face. "I am grateful for Mr. Ridley's presence."

"Very good, my lady." The butler nodded. "If you should need anything else, please ring." He cast a curious glance at Mr. Ridley. "Thank you for assisting her."

The former Bow Street man inclined his chin. Only once the butler departed the room did he choose to speak. "I should go. There is work to be done and—"

"No." Taking refuge in her tea, Theodosia swallowed a hearty sip. "We need to find Jacob, so I want you to stay. Have tea with me." Her hand holding the teacup trembled. "Until my son comes home, you and I are going to spend every waking hour together. Because we are partners in this." She sighed when he looked skeptical. "We shall have a council of war to regroup." With a hand, she waved him into a nearby chair. "Sit, Mr. Ridley. I can be rather demanding if the occasion allows."

"So I am beginning to realize." Unexpectedly, a chuckle came from him, and the rich, smokey sound sent shivers of appreciation down her spine. "Council of war, eh?" He took up residence in the chair she'd indicated. "Interesting term."

Theodosia shrugged. She set down her cup in order to prepare one for him. "It is something my brother says. Fitting here, no?"

"Indeed." And he watched her with those penetrating eyes that gave nothing of his thoughts away.

Chapter Six

Well, damn. What the devil had possessed him to kiss her?

Hudson frowned into the contents of his teacup as their conversation dwindled once more into silence. Not the awkward kind that one wishes to find an immediate escape from, but more of a companionable pause where two people are comfortable in each other's company. It was all too domestic, and very much tempting.

Of course he knew exactly why he'd kissed her. It hadn't been a proper kiss, merely a peck if one wished for the truth. But she'd looked so vulnerable and lost, and though she'd striven to remain strong in the face of an enormous horror, the fact she could still laugh and smile occasionally drew him to her like a moth to a flame.

So, he'd kissed her, to see if those rose-colored lips were as pillowy soft as he suspected — they were — and to give her a modicum of comfort.

And because he hadn't been motivated to anything of the sort with a woman in far too long. The fact this slender viscountess with curves in the right places and eyes that could send men to war had managed to burrow under his skin in such a short period of time surprised him. Never had he known a similar reaction to a client before.

Suddenly, he wished there was something much stronger in his cup than tea.

"Why did you come to Rome, Mr. Ridley?"

As soon as he raised his head, his gaze collided with hers. Those shimmering gray-blue depths beckoned him closer. *Christ*, being so close to her, spending time in her company was going to be the death of him if he wasn't careful. "I retired from Bow Street."

The viscountess sipped her tea and watched him from over the rim of her cup. "I doubt that is the only reason."

"It is not." When a bottle of brandy didn't suddenly appear on the tea tray merely because he wished it, Hudson sighed and sipped his ordinary tea, unadulterated by cream or sugar. Her raised eyebrows put forth far too many questions he wasn't sure he wished to answer at this time, but she was obviously expecting... something. And perhaps he owed it to her after what she'd shared earlier on their walk. "My last case went horribly wrong. I was reprimanded.

While I nursed my wounds, both physical and mental, I decided I didn't want to hold that position any longer."

Her gaze strayed to the side of his face. "Do you wish to talk about it?"

"Not particularly." He lifted his free hand, traced the scars with a fingertip, willed his mind *not* to return to that day and gruesome scene. "Perhaps I'll share at another time."

"I hope you do." The lady's lips turned down ever so slightly with a pout that had him stifling any sort of reaction, for suddenly, that brief, chaste kiss hadn't been nearly enough to satisfy his curiosity about her. "Is it me you don't trust, or everyone?"

Interesting question, and one he'd asked himself time out of hand. "Out of all the people I've ever come into contact with, you are one of the more upstanding ones. Given the chance, I would trust you implicitly." And that didn't happen often or easily. He drained the contents of his teacup. "However, you are a beautiful creature with secrets in your eyes and confliction in your soul. *That* is something I wonder about."

What hadn't she told him, and would it be the key to unlocking the mystery of this case? He didn't press, for she was already emotional enough. If he waited long enough, usually a client would tell him everything.

"I appreciate that, but sometimes there are things even a former Bow Street man doesn't wish to know." When she smiled, it reflected in her eyes, which was the first time it had done that since they'd met and came accompanied by a pretty blush in her cheeks. "Would you care for more tea?"

"I would. Thank you." With his cup in hand, he leaned forward with the vessel extended. As she poured out a measure of the amber liquid, he studied her in profile. Blonde hair that shone in the sun that streamed into the room from the windows. Tiny lines that framed the corners of her eyes signaling the fact she'd laughed and smiled much in her time as a mother. The hand that shook slightly while she returned the teapot to the tray. The curve of her pale cheek that almost begged for the cup of his hand. Would that he could take her away from everything that brought her anxiety and let her spend her time idle so the sun could kiss her skin.

With a refresh of her own cup, Lady Ballantyne raised her gaze to his. "When you decided to retire, why did you choose Rome? Surely there are other areas of the world that are closer to London you find fascinating."

"I had considered that." Hudson leaned back in his chair, resting an ankle on a knee. "However, seaside attractions at Brighton didn't interest me at the time; neither did taking the waters at Bath." He uttered a half-snort half-chuckle when he thought of himself in either of those areas. "Besides, I was rather out of charity with England so thought it was the perfect time to pull up stakes, start over elsewhere."

"You didn't find it painful to wrench away from your roots?"

He took refuge in a swallow of tea. "My parents have been dead for over ten years. Perished when a fire consumed a line of row houses—theirs among them. I have a younger brother, but the last time I had a letter from him, he was content in working as an East India man and wasn't ready to leave Bombay."

It had been an age since he'd last heard from Jameson, younger than he by two years. But then, he'd only recently told his sibling that he'd relocated to Rome. They had never been close; and every once in a while he wondered if he ought not try to resurrect a relationship that had never solidified.

It hadn't been a priority, but as of late, the need to have family around him—however thin the connection—had grown strong.

"So, to answer your question, Lady Ballantyne, there are no roots for me to speak of. Rome seemed fairly interesting after reading a few travel journals, and the idea of friendly sunshine, for touring cathedrals and ruins was too great to leave to idle wondering."

She nibbled on a tiny seed cake, and with every bite, Hudson stared at her mouth, stopping his thoughts just as they converged to a point of jealousy of that confection. "Did you know the Trevi Fountain is one of my most favorite places in the city?"

"Ah, I know that spot well." He offered her a small smile. "I have been there many times when I need a place for contemplation or to cool my feet if the crowds are low."

"I never would have thought you'd be one for public bathing, Mr. Ridley." Humor wove through her voice. "A proper man such as yourself would no doubt frown at the people who do such things."

Interesting, that. "Do you take the occasional dip in the waters, then."

The faint blush returned to her cheeks. "If the day is warm enough and the crowds are thin." One shoulder lifted with a shrug. "There are worse ways to stay cool or find a bit of fun."

"Oh, indeed." How did she find her fun when she wasn't filling all her time being a mother? But he didn't wish to ask and disturb the fragile friendship springing between them. "In any event, I came to Rome. Where many English people tend to favor destinations in the north such as Genoa, Milan, and especially Venice for its scenic splendors, pleasures, and public spectacles, I felt a kindred connection of sorts with Rome and its inhabitants." He once more drained his teacup. "There is history here that's both rich with power and full of cautionary tales. Treasure to be had, of course, but also much food for thought and sights that enrich the soul as well as the spirit."

Slowly, she nodded. "Everyone is so congenial here. Eventually, I would like to tour through the Naples area. I have heard stories waxing nearly poetic regarding the food and the hospitality. My brother is acquaintances with the British envoy to the region, so I could arrange travel through him."

Seeing the sights along the way. Soaking up the Mediterranean sunshine. Bearing witness to how she interacted with peoples of different regions and showing her child the ruins. Then he reined in his thoughts. *You are not with her for any other reason save finding said child.* "Yes, that would be quite the trip, and one I'd be anxious to take as well." He set the teacup on a small round table at his elbow. "I have been told there is the remains of a temple to a goddess set on a hillside in the Vesuvius region. Eventually, I would like to see that area if only to feel kindred with the people of Pompei who perished when the volcano erupted."

She nodded. "Can you imagine what those poor inhabitants felt like when the night turned into fire and their world ended?"

"Try as I might, I cannot. It must have been a terrifying prospect." He frowned, and then let himself get temporarily lost in thought. "Each time I visit a historical site, I have the tendency to think about the past civilizations that had lived and worked in that area."

"Or loved," she added in a small voice. "To be there and know your life was over and the world as they knew it was doomed?" Her voice broke. "If that happened to me, I would like to hope I was with the people I loved best, holding onto them at the last."

"It is a lovely thought. Something we should always aspire to." Dancing on the edge of maudlin thoughts, he forcefully pushed them away. Then a chuckle escaped him. "Perhaps it's my mind being overactive or bored with nothing much to occupy it."

"You have my son's case."

"That I do, and trust me, he is never far from my thoughts." Did she think him a cad?

"Good" The viscountess allowed a small smile. "Though England is full of history as well, it is of a different variety than is what's found on the Italian peninsula." She sighed and left her own cup on the table in front of her. "The sad thing? I never knew how much I haven't done in my time in Rome until my son went missing." The delicate tendons of her neck worked with a hard swallow. Those blue-gray eyes implored him, whether she was aware of the emotion or not. "We *must* find Jacob, Mr. Ridley."

"I agree with you on that point." He rose to his feet as the restless energy of before returned. Clasping his hands behind his back,

Hudson began to pace. "Perhaps you should refer to me as Hudson. A kidnapping case and the need to spend copious hours together to solve it shouldn't necessitate enduring formality." Truth be told, he merely wished to hear his Christian name in her dulcet tones. "And if things go wrong, I would rather you hate me as Hudson than Mr. Ridley." There was every possibility both could occur.

Something flickered over her face, but he couldn't identify it. "Though I rather doubt that will happen, I suppose removing the formality *would* be cozier." She tilted her head slightly as she glanced at him, or rather he had the sense that she evaluated him. Would he come up lacking? "You may call me Theodosia."

"I look forward to doing so." God, even her name was lovely and mysterious. If he wasn't careful, he would fall beneath her spell, and that would prove disastrous, both for him and this case. To cover his confusion, Hudson resumed pacing. It didn't matter how they chose to address each other; such things wouldn't help to bring her son back. If he could perhaps understand her on a deeper level, it might unlock the missing pieces he lacked. "Do you have a recent rendering or painting of your son?"

"Oh, yes!" She sprang up from the sofa, made her way about the room to a curio cabinet, and then she brought forth an oval frame painted in gilt. "This was done the last Christmastide we had with Nathaniel." Sadness clouded her eyes. "It is one of the only pieces I have with all of us together."

"Ah." Gently, he pulled the frame from her fingers while she returned to her spot on the sofa. Perhaps eight inches in height, the oil painting portrayed her seated on a delicate chair. The wine-colored gown brought out the subtle pink undertones in her skin. Behind her with a hand on her shoulder stood a man Hudson assumed was the viscount—her husband. Handsome in an understated way, Lord Ballantyne had a disarming grin, his chestnut hair had been done in a popular style, and his collar points weren't overly high. Sitting on his knees at Theodosia's feet, wearing his own little jacket and waistcoat was a then five-year-old Jacob. His blond hair wasn't as pure or glimmering as Theodosia's, but he seemed a naturally happy child and had looked at the artist with a bit of mischief in his hazel eyes. "He is quite a taking thing."

But the longer he stared at the portrait, the more confused he became. Despite the fact they were definitely a cohesive family, the boy didn't resemble either of his parents. Perhaps, then, he took after his grandparents.

"Thank you for this." He laid the portrait on a nearby table. "Tell me what your greatest fears are… Theodosia." Damn, that felt all too good saying her name aloud.

You are in danger of being the world's biggest nodcock.

"I think I am living one of them as we speak." She sent a last, lingering glance at the remains of the tea service before finally resting her gaze on him. "I fear losing my son." Her voice broke on the last word. "He is all but lost now, and still we are no closer to finding him than we were when he didn't return to the courtyard."

"These things take time." He didn't know how to comfort her, not without touching her. Words would only go so far, and hadn't he already said them? Besides, in his experience, he knew the probability of the outcome not being what she wanted. There would only be agony and grief that followed.

"Of course I know that." She waved a hand in apparent frustration. "As I sit here talking to you, I am seething inside, Hudson."

He refrained from putting a hand over his heart at the sound of his name coming from her lips. Never had anything been as meaningful. Instead, raw need shuddered through him, awakening his shaft, and for the first time in many months, he felt an interest in a woman. "That is how it usually goes."

"Well, how would I know that?" The bite and snap in her voice betrayed her mental state.

"This is the first time my son has been kidnapped!" She tossed her head, and the stubbornness he was beginning to see from her came further out. "There are no clues. I hired you but to no avail, apparently." A huff escaped. "I thought when Nathaniel died my world had ended, but that pain was nothing to what I'm feeling now, and quite frankly I am so... angry and... lost, and somehow I feel this is my fault."

Well, damn. Despite himself, Hudson drifted closer to her location, almost laid a hand on her shoulder, but held himself back. The attraction sparking between them would hinder the investigation, and he didn't need more guilt. "Many people in your position feel that way. They examine every moment of their lives that lead up to the second their loved ones were taken to see if they made a misstep, but that's not how any of it works." When her chin quivered, his chest tightened. "There are evil men and women in this world, bent on destruction and malice. You were just unfortunate enough to be caught up in the middle of that."

"Bah." Theodosia looked away, but there was no mistaking the well of tears in her eyes. "There are far too many of such men in this world, men who have so much excess they cannot trouble themselves to care for the weak or needful."

What an odd thing to say, but then, she was overwrought. "I understand." Going against his every instinct, Hudson sat next to her on the sofa. The warmth of her called out to him, but he ignored it; had to. "That is why I'm here. I want to help, but we both need to grasp at hope. It won't do to declare defeat so soon."

"I am trying." She reached out a hand, and he would be a nodcock not to take it in his, wrap his fingers about hers, rub his thumb along her knuckles and hope to God it brought her a modicum of comfort. "If I lose my son, I will be alone, and I fear being forgotten over everything else." Those blue-gray eyes would haunt him for all the emotion clouding them. "How horrible would that be?"

"That is one of my deepest fears as well," he admitted in a soft voice. "After all the good work that I have done, will anyone remember me for changing those lives?" He stared at her as his fears and insecurities rose up like specters in the dark. "And when I allow that to enter into my mind, it brings with it other fears. What if I can no longer help people with my skills? What if I never had them to begin with?"

Bloody hell, why did I tell her that?

Compassion lined her face. "It is quite all right to let others see you are vulnerable." Theodosia turned toward him and clasped his other hand in hers. "In fact, it makes you more relatable and your clients will be more apt to trust you."

"Perhaps." Despite his resolve to keep his feelings aloof, he leaned toward her. "It is a strange thing."

"Agreed." She tightened her hold on his hands, and she leaned toward him as well. Her gaze drifted to his mouth, and another surge of raw desire went through him. "I am losing control of everything I once knew, and the more I try to fight it, the worse it grows." Uncertainty scudded through her eyes. "What am I supposed to do once I fully break?"

The poor thing. "Sometimes, we all must break in order to find out how strong we truly are. Only then can we build ourselves into something better with a clearer head." God, but he hoped that were true, for he had been waiting over two years to become a better version of himself.

To once more be a hero.

She was close enough to him now that the warmth of her breath skated over his lips. "What happens if I break and start to fall?"

The whisper was both thrilling and so frightening he wished to run from this house and the pressure currently resting upon his shoulders. Tightening his hold on her hands, he said, "I promise I'll be there to catch you."

If fate were kind, he wouldn't fail again.

Chapter Seven

Theodosia's pulse fluttered in time to the butterfly ballet in her belly. Oh, what was it about this man that pulled her into his web and made her forget—even temporarily—about the horror of her current situation?

To that end, what sort of woman was she that she craved that tiny bit of insanity in the midst of the tragedy missing her son had become? *I need to know none of this is my fault and that it will all come out right in the end.* And oh, she wanted to bury herself in Hudson's strength for a few moments, to rest while she gathered her own.

Afterward, she was never certain of who moved first, but one second, they were sitting beside each other on the sofa holding hands and the next she was nearly on his lap, pressing her lips to his with one hand resting on his chest while the other she twined about his nape.

With a groan, Hudson kissed her back. He slipped a hand to the small of her back, pulling her as close as he could with them remaining in their original positions. Then he cupped her cheek, feathered his fingers into her hair and tilted up her chin to better deepen the embrace. Need twisted with excitement down her spine. It had been such a long time since she'd felt wanted by anyone outside a capacity as a mother or a sister. The sensations went straight to her head as if she'd ingested a half bottle of champagne on an empty stomach.

With the veriest of pressure on his nape, she guided him to where she needed him to be and kissed him, showed him how she enjoyed being kissed. The dear man took the hint with glorious alacrity, and with a simple slant of his mouth over hers, he drew the tip of his tongue along the seam of her lips. When she opened and he found her tongue with his, her hold on reality tumbled even further.

"This sets a dangerous precedent," he whispered seconds before he dragged his lips beneath her jaw, nibbling and licking her skin until he discovered a particular spot that made her almost purr with pleasure. "And it's highly unprofessional on my part."

She curled a hand into his lapel and wished he'd stop talking and kiss her again. "Yet I hired you. Doesn't that mean you should look after my emotional well-being as well? Isn't that part of solving the case?" *Oh, goodness!* He drew his lips down the column of her throat merely to tease the space between her collarbones with his tongue. How was that patch of skin so erotically sensitive?

"I am not certain that is how it works." He returned to her lips and took possession of them as if he were always meant to be there.

Hunger and need burned through her in a hot wave. Though she wanted nothing more than to crawl into his lap and continue kissing him until she felt safe and protected and ready once again to take up the mantle of courage, she couldn't quite forget that she was a lady and he was a former Bow Street man given the task of locating her missing son, but oh how she wanted to break, to fall, to let him catch her and perhaps put her back together again.

In any event, it didn't matter, for the discreet clearing of a masculine throat at the door had her springing apart from him as if she'd been burned and he the fire that had done it. When she glanced up, she frowned as the butler came into the room bearing a small silver salver in one hand. A small wooden box rested atop it. "What is it, Carruthers?" If there was a fair amount of pique in her inquiry, and a certain breathlessness, she couldn't help it, for she had been interrupted before the embrace had time to ripen into something highly appealing.

With a curious glance at Hudson, the butler came forward while Theodosia rose to her feet. "A missive and package were just delivered for you, my lady."

"From whom?" The investigator was right there at her side, and the rumble of his voice in her ear gave her a modicum of comfort. He met her gaze. "This could be a possible break in the case."

Anticipation and dread warred for dominance in her belly. She nodded but said nothing, merely took the ivory envelope from the salver while Hudson confiscated the box. "Thank you, Carruthers. You may go."

"Very good, my lady." He shot Hudson another interested glance, but when the other man didn't give anything away, the butler departed the room.

"Do you think this is a ransom note from the kidnappers?" The hand holding the envelope trembled, but she eyed the box with equal trepidation.

"It's a good possibility, but we won't know until you open the letter." He gently shook the small box. "Shall I do the same with this?"

"Yes, please." Theodosia broke the plain wax seal. She flipped up the flap of the envelope and then slid a folded sheet of paper out while Hudson manipulated the twine around the wooden box. Then she gawked as he pulled a rectangular-shaped emerald from a bed of straw, and she would wager everything she had it was the same 43 carat gemstone that used to belong to her husband. "Oh, dear."

"Indeed." He held the stone up, and the play of sunlight glimmered and refracted off its cut and beveled surfaces. "Was this what your boy was playing with before he disappeared?"

"Yes." She could hardly force the word out from a tight throat. Not able to look at Hudson, she focused on the letter which she unfolded.

Lady Ballantyne,

I have no need of baubles, so you may have the emerald back. It is your son I want, and you know why. Revenge is sweet, no matter how many years have passed. Next time stay out of affairs that do not concern you.

Do not think to find the boy else I have no qualms in making certain you join your husband. Jacob will remain with me here until the end of the fifteenth when we depart for England.

And he will have the life he was born to.

Hanneford

The breath whooshed from Theodosia's lungs. *Oh, dear God.* She crushed the stationery in her hand as she curled her fingers into a fist. Except, when she and Nathaniel had found Jacob as a tiny, barely week-old baby beneath a bush in Hyde Park—where Doris had deposited him on orders from the Marquess of Hanneford—that life would have ended in a premature death.

What did he mean for the boy now?

To say nothing of the way the missive was cryptically worded. Had the marquess orchestrated Nathaniel's death? Instead of a random mugging on the street that did, was it by an assassin's knife that her husband had met his fate?

"Surely that wasn't the case..." For if it was, the situation was more dire than she'd ever thought.

"Theodosia?" Concern hung from that one-word inquiry as Hudson eyed her with both speculation and suspicion. "Is all well?"

"I don't... No." Emotion grew thick in her throat. Fright played her spine as if it had nothing else to do. Then it turned into cold terror that gripped her insides and ceased her lungs, preventing her from drawing a deep breath. "This is rapidly getting out of hand," she finally whispered as the envelope fluttered to the floor.

Hudson set the box and the emerald on a small table then held out his right hand. "Might I see the letter? All the blood has drained from your face. I would know the reason why, for I suspect this is a missing piece of the puzzle I need to solve your case."

"Oh." With her heartbeat slamming through her veins and that damned darkness encroaching upon the edges of her vision, she stared at the investigator. Though she knew he merely wanted to help, and she had hired him for exactly that, he couldn't be party to this huge lie, he just couldn't. He would judge her, look at her with disdain in his eyes, and his opinion of her would shift. *I cannot have that.* A few retreating steps put much needed distance between them. "This is my mess, and now perhaps I am reaping the consequences of a certain action Nathaniel and I made."

Then because she was a coward at heart, Theodosia turned tail and ran from the room — from Hudson — and the only thing she wished to do was hide and sob out the anguish building in her heart. How were actions from the past haunting her future?

Panic guided her footsteps, and as she left the house, running blindly along the streets in the noon day sun as if she had no more dignity than someone with a fallen reputation, fear joined the efforts until her pulse pounded and confusion clouded her brain. Tears filled her eyes, but she kept moving forward, not knowing her direction or destination. She couldn't stop —

shouldn't stop—for in doing so she would have to face the sin she'd committed all those years ago even if it had been for the right reasons.

To face the harsh realities doing so had made her forget.

The cloying darkness hovered on the edge of her vision, creeping ever closer in on consciousness in the quest to devour her whole. Wouldn't that just be so ironic if she collapsed on a public street so that everyone would know of her shame? And still she ran until her lungs heaved with the effort of trying to breathe and stave off fainting into blissful oblivion.

Only when her strength had given out and she had no more energy within her to continue did she collapse to a grassy courtyard of an unfamiliar building. Falling to her knees without regard to the fabric of her gown, Theodosia finally gave into the sobs that had threatened ever since Jacob went missing. Before she covered her face in her hands and let emotion have at her, she tucked the crumpled note into her bodice.

Oh, why had her husband been torn from her life and side when she needed him so much right now? Never had she felt as lonely in her widowhood as she did in this moment.

Then a familiar hand was on her shoulder, and the scents of cedarwood and orange wafted to her nose. Hudson had come after her. Of course he would be the one to offer her comfort when she needed it the most. "Can I assume the missive you received had sinister overtones and that you know exactly why?" There was no censure in those inquires, only mild interest and overwhelming kindness.

"Oh, dear." Warmth went through her chest as she looked up at him. Backlit by the sun, he was naught but a large form that offered her a temporary shield from that same sunshine. "Please leave me to my fate. I deserve it."

"I rather doubt that." He moved into her line of sight, and then dropped to one knee before her. Those intense eyes of his bored into her, and so easily she could rest in those ice blue pools if only she would let herself. "For all I have observed of you, there isn't a malicious bone in your body."

"Ha, perhaps not, but just now, I wish to kill the man who has taken my son." The words, though softly spoken, echoed with fierce determination and ire.

He took her hand. "Tell me." The investigative part of him warred with the compassion for the situation; she saw it in his face, and that endeared him to her more than anything else. Hudson Ridley was a man of his word and a man of honor. He wouldn't stop until the job had been done. "Let me help, even in this."

The comforting baritone sought to batter the walls she'd erected about herself when

Nathaniel had died. His presence only served to distract and discomfit as much as it pleased her. "Oh, Hudson." What would she do in this moment without him? "I wish I could tell you, but I'm a horrible person. This," she vaguely waved a hand to mean everything that had happened, "is all my fault. Mine and Nathaniel's, and now I'm afraid he has paid the price for that... with me not far behind."

Who would look after Jacob then? The marquess' household wasn't the place for a sensitive, inquisitive boy like him, even if that man was Jacob's true father.

For long moments, Hudson regarded her. He ignored the curious stares from the faces that appeared in the windows of the building in front of them, and all the while, the constant pressure of his fingers clasping hers kept her grounded. "Perhaps or perhaps not, but this isn't the proper venue to discuss such matters. Too many prying eyes and gossiping lips."

Finally, she glanced about the area, and try as she might, she didn't recognize the neighbors. "I don't want to go home. I..." As a new deluge of tears overcame her, she shook her head. "Please. I don't need Thomas getting word and coming back there, to either coddle or lecture me."

"Understandable." The ghost of a grin took possession of his mouth, and oh how she wished he would kiss her again. "I will take you to my home." She must have looked as shocked as she felt, for his grin widened. "You can have tea—or brandy if you require stronger fortification—for both will calm your nerves. Whatever you choose, we will talk, but I need to know what *you* know, and why you feel it has bearing on this case."

She brushed at the moisture on her cheeks with her free hand. Already, there was a bit of a crowd forming on the street nearby. What a coil. "There is no way out for me, I fear."

"Let *me* decide that." For a large man, he rose gracefully to his feet and assisted her into a standing position as he did so. "Besides, we are not far from my boarding house." When she eyed him askance, he shrugged. "You ran for a while, and the remainder of the walk will do you good."

The world spun about her, and the darkness at the edges of her vision hadn't dissipated fully, so when she swayed on her feet, he was there and wrapped an arm about her waist to keep her upright. Heat went through her cheeks. "I apologize. Every time I am afraid or feeling panic or overwhelmed, I have the tendency to faint. It has been that way ever since I first made my Come Out into society."

A rumbling chuckle sounded deep in his chest before the sound released into the air. "What a delightful detail."

She fell into step beside him. Relief twisted down her spine. "You don't find it a weakness?" It was something she'd always been embarrassed about.

"Not at all. Every person has a defense mechanism in order to guard against bad news." He slid her a glance and the corners of his lips twitched. "But perhaps there are ways we can practice taking in such news that might prevent you from passing out at inopportune times."

The fact he'd said "we" sent a rush of heat through her chest. "The only time I seem to forget about those fears is on a dance floor."

"Oh? Do you enjoy taking such exercise?"

"Oddly enough, I do. Cares and concerns melt away when I'm busy concentrating on the steps to each set." She couldn't help but give him a grin. "And all the better if the male company is congenial and powerful."

"Interesting." His Adam's apple bobbed with a hard swallow. "I can't say that I've danced more than three times in my entire life."

"We must remedy that." What would it feel like being ushered about a floor in his arms? Needing to change the subject, she said, "I had no idea you resided within walking distance of the ambassador's residence." In fact, many of the villas that dotted the hillside street where her brother's villa lay housed various ambassadors and dignitaries. It made for an eclectic area and one that always brought her joy.

"When it comes down to brass tacks, Rome isn't that large at all." He guided her down a charming, quiet street. Somewhere in the distance, the ring of children's laughter drifted to her ears, and with it came another wave of guilt. "Here we are. Mrs. Claudian's boarding house. This is where I've called home since arriving in Rome."

"I vaguely remember from last night, but it was too dark to see correctly."

The building was as unassuming as the man, and she liked the spread of ivy over the brickwork. Perhaps she'd have a glimpse into Hudson's life behind the persona of the former Bow Street officer. "If you are certain?" If the scandalbroth of her visiting a bachelor man's rooms got back to Thomas, there would be hell to pay.

"I have the best intentions, of course. I have met with a few clients in my drawing room or parlor, and that is where I first met you, if you'll recall."

"I do." Another round of heat went through her cheeks.

He chuckled again. "If you wish for everything to remain proper, we can utilize Mrs. Claudian's public parlor." He held open the front door for her precede him. "Don't be surprised if she wishes to join in on the conversation, though."

The opportunity to see his inner sanctum and be alone with him was too great a temptation, as was being hidden away from prying eyes. "I am quite capable of making decisions for my own life. Thank you, Mr. Ridley. Please proceed." She took refuge behind a haughty tone, for being in his company, missing the feeling of his arm about her waist as they trod a narrow entry hall, had her at sixes and sevens.

"Ah, thank you for putting me in my place, Lady Ballantyne." Humor wove through his voice, and she didn't mind the return to formality while they could be overheard. "The stairs are just past the parlor there on the left." However, when they would have passed the doorway, someone within called his name. "Well, shit," he murmured beneath his breath.

"What is it?" she whispered and sought out his gaze, wondering what was wrong.

"My landlady, Mrs. Claudian." Consternation filled his expression. "Best have this over with, but don't be surprised if she attempts a bit of matchmaking," he said in a low voice as he escorted her into the room. "Apparently, every day I remain single upsets her spirit."

Theodosia couldn't help but giggle at his aggrieved tones. "Hush. She's probably protective of you." Then she smiled at the matronly woman who rose up from a sofa. An embroidery project lay on a nearby cushion.

"What is this, Mr. Ridley? You have found a pretty lady friend?" The landlady swept across the floor with a hand outstretched. She clasped one of Theodosia's and gave her a wide grin. "Welcome. I am Mrs. Claudian. Looking after this one," she hooked the thumb of her free hand over her shoulder at Hudson, "is a chore. Stubborn man. Terrible housekeeper."

Now that was an interesting insight. "Hullo. I am Lady Ballantyne." The affection between them was obvious and made her feel as if she were with family.

"She is a client, Mrs. Claudian," Hudson explained with a patient expression that put her in mind of a frustrated son who had an overly pushy mother. "You should be happy. Aren't you forever reminding me I still have talent?" When the other woman tsked her tongue, he nodded. "Her son is missing."

Gently, Theodosia pulled her hand from the other woman's. "Mr. Ridley is doing his best to solve the case." *Except, I have hindered that investigation.* Oh, Hudson would be so angry when she finally told him the truth, because she would. It was inevitable.

"He is good at what he does." The older lady bounced her gaze between them. "In many ventures, no doubt." She sent a speaking glance her way. "Are you a widow?" When Theodosia's lower jaw dropped, Mrs. Claudian clicked her tongue. "He is attractive, no? Big and strong. Nice shoulders. Probably well hung."

"Mrs. Claudian!" Embarrassed anger ran through Hudson's exclamation.

"Ah, hit a nerve." She winked while Theodosia's cheeks burned anew. Now that the picture had entered her mind, she couldn't evict it. "He can comfort you in this trying time, yes? My husband always said a round in the sheets was good for the mind. And spirt."

A fit of coughing assailed Hudson. When he finally got hold of himself, he cleared his throat. Consternation reflected in his eyes, for the landlady or for thinking they were compatible *that way*? "That is quite enough, Mrs. Claudian. Our guest is a lady."

"What? A woman's status in society means nothing. Sex is sex. Even the gods chased after it." The matron shrugged and looked at him with a baffled expression. Truly, Italians were freer about such things than the English. "Widows have needs, and she is perfect in form." With her hands, the landlady made an outline of a woman's body as if it were an hourglass. "She is emotional. Hold her. Talk to her beyond the case." She pushed at Hudson's arm. "Whatever happens... happens."

"Oh, dear God." He looked at Theodosia. A red flush had risen above his collar. "I apologize for her plain speech. She has trouble with boundaries."

Mrs. Claudian snorted. "Too reserved. Let down the hair, Mr. Ridley."

Though amusing, it was a tad uncomfortable only for the fact that she'd had those same thoughts regarding the investigator at one time or another. "Hush. She's adorable." With a wink of her own, Theodosia gave the other woman a smile. "He *is* lovely, and I know you take very good care of him."

"I try." Pleasure lined the older lady's face. "He is like my own son."

Hudson huffed with apparent frustration. "She is nosy and intrusive."

"It means she cares." Theodosia glanced at him, and when she met his gaze, acute need shivered down her spine. What would it be like to lay with this man?

"He resists taking that next step." The land lady tsked. "Bullheaded Englishman. Thinks himself too damaged and ugly for a woman to want."

"What a ridiculous notion." The scars had taken her aback at first, of course, but they only served to give him character, perhaps distinction.

"Agreed." In her charming way, Mrs. Claudian took Theodosia's hand and put it into Hudson's. Heated tingles danced up to her elbow. "He needs to marry. Make him a better man. Less of a sour puss." She waggled her bushy eyebrows as she looked at her. "And you should have many babies, my lady. Beautiful, chubby babies that will make the man smile and melt."

Heat again slapped at Theodosia's cheeks, but it was accompanied by infinite sadness. "My first priority is finding my son." She couldn't look at Hudson. A couple of kisses didn't make a relationship, and even if it did, he was well below her in station. If that ended up not mattering, no doubt he would wish to have a family, and that was something she couldn't provide him. Panic climbed her throat and darkness invaded the edges of her vision. It was why she and Nathaniel had rescued Jacob to begin with.

Ever aware of her changing moods, Hudson cleared his throat. "If you will excuse us, Mrs. Claudian? The lady is exhausted and has received some rather upsetting news prior to arriving here. She needs to rest."

"Rest." The older woman rolled her eyes heavenward. "That is *not* what she needs and is a poor use of a bed, but if you are too stupid to know, I won't tell you."

Hysterical laughter rushed into Theodosia's throat. "A bed with fluffy goose down feather pillows," she said in a sing song voice. She could almost feel the weight of his body on top of hers, pressing her into the mattress as he explored her skin with his tongue… If she didn't leave this room, she'd faint dead away while honking like a loon. "It was lovely to meet you."

The landlady nodded. "I hope Mr. Ridley's gruff exterior doesn't run you off but fear not. He *will* find your son." She looked upon him with the love of a mother. "He is talented, this one." Then she transferred her attention to Theodosia. "In more ways than one, hmm? Perhaps you will discover that too."

"Bloody hell. Damned interfering woman," Hudson muttered as he slipped a hand about her upper arm. "Quickly, now. I'm on the second floor. We'd better go before she's hustling us off to the nearest church altar."

That struck her as funny, so she laughed but she wondered if the mirth wasn't inappropriate for the occasion. After all, Jacob was still missing, and she was rapidly falling apart. It was only a matter of time before Hudson convinced her to hand over the letter, yet the only thing she could think about was relieving him of his clothing and losing herself in a hot, sweaty bout of raw, mindless intercourse.

After that, everything would be lost, and there would be no more use in clinging to the carefully fabricated story she'd spun about her life.

Chapter Eight

Damn Mrs. Claudian!

Hudson fumed as he escorted Theodosia along the narrow corridor and then up the narrow wooden staircase at the back of the house. The swish of her hips as she went before him scattered his concentration; her scent of lilacs strained the edges of his control. What must she think of him after his landlady's penchant for plain speaking? After that about of poorly disguised hints, all he could think about was taking the viscountess to bed.

Was a bit of seduction the key to encouraging her to tell him all her secrets?

"Last door on the left." The utterance sounded overly loud in the empty corridor. At this time of the day, everyone had come home for the midday meal, and following that, would take a couple of hours to relax or nap while the heat of the afternoon began to build. Perfect time to tease out Theodosia's past or would it be too much a risk because they might be overhead? Never had he contemplated his neighbors' comings and goings so much. "I apologize in advance that my space isn't as tidy as you are no doubt accustomed to." Trepidation built in his gut, for it had been more than a few months since he'd willingly invited a woman into his personal rooms. "I don't have a maid, though Mrs. Claudian comes in once a week and does spot cleaning. I suspect she rather thinks I'm hopeless."

"Stop. Your landlady cares for you as she would a son."

"Her children are all grown and from what I've understood, they are busy with their own lives."

"Ah. That makes sense." Theodosia nodded. "Life is not meant to be lived in austere settings without our favorite and most comfortable things around us." She waited at the door while he fumbled in a waistcoat pocket for the key. "I wish I would have learned that lesson much sooner," she admitted in a soft voice. "Being a viscountess would have perhaps been a less demanding endeavor, and perhaps I wouldn't have been so uptight, so cautious..."

Obviously, the woman labored beneath a fair amount of anxiety to the point of making herself sick or having fainting spells. Why the devil was she always worried and fearful? And more to the point, what the hell had been written in that letter which had spooked her into flight?

Not knowing the answers to either question, Hudson manipulated the lock on his door and then quickly swung the panel open. Yes, she required something to help her relax and trust him, but would doing just that make her pull farther away from him? Pocketing his key, he stepped aside and let Theodosia go into the apartment before him, then he gently closed the door behind them, being sure to throw the lock lest his landlady bustle in uninvited.

Not that a locked door would stop her. But if she thought they were up here making full use of a perfectly good bed…

Damn you, Mrs. Claudian, for even putting the idea front and center in my brain.

"Oh, and be advised." But his warning came too late, for the unmistakable sound of a feline growl echoed in the air. Gooseflesh marched along his flesh. "I have a cat. Her name is Luna, and she isn't fond of most people."

"Thank you for telling me." Theodosia eyed the mostly white cat as she joined them in the drawing room. "How pretty you are," she told the feline, but true to form, Luna ignored the outstretched hand, eyed their guest with disdain and walked a wide circle around her in order to reach his location. "Ah. I can see where her loyalty lies."

"Yes, well, she's protective ever since I rescued her as a kitten on my first day in Rome."

"What a lovely thing to do." When the viscountess wandered through the drawing room, she frowned at the hole where the chair and ottoman used to be, but she said nothing. "There are no personal touches in this room." It wasn't a question.

"I am a private man, and besides, anything personal is in my past." He bent to scratch Luna behind her ears then when the cat skittered away presumably into the smaller bedroom, he trailed after Theodosia. "There is no use in dwelling on things no longer here."

"That is a sad narrative." She went from table to shelf, examining objects and looking at bric-a-brac. "There are lessons to learn from our pasts and making ourselves feel that pain — or whatever emotion — can allow us to grow."

Interesting that she introduced such a subject. "Then why won't you let yourself revisit *your* past? What are you afraid of?"

"The answer is easy, my dear Mr. Ridley." Turning about, she held his gaze with her. Tears shimmered in those gray-blue depths, magnifying the color. "Everything."

The urge to protect her welled strong. She wasn't doing well as the case progressed, and he desperately wanted to know the contents of that letter. "When things seem overwhelming, the best advice I can offer is to address the little items first until you can reach the heart of the matter."

"My son is safe, if probably confused and frightened," she said without preamble, but she was obviously still upset, for she laced her fingers together and clasped them tightly in front of her. "And until the fifteenth of this month, he will be in Rome. After that?" She shrugged and a few tears fell to her cheeks. "I don't know."

Immediately on the alert, Hudson swiftly closed the distance between them. That vulnerability, that confusion, that utter desolation she exhibited was as powerful as any aphrodisiac, for he could help her if she would just let him in. "Where is he?" When she didn't answer, he took possession of her hands. "Theodosia, where is Jacob? Who has taken him? And how do you know that?"

"I..." She shook her head. When she would have tugged her hands from his hold, he tightened his grip. "It's complicated and I don't wish to talk about it at this time."

With a growl of both need and frustration, Hudson cupped her cheek and jaw, encouraged her head to tip slightly backward, and their gazes to meet. "What *do* you want then?"

Those moisture spiked lashes framed round eyes, and the longer he watched, the darker the irises grew. Her plush lips parted in anticipation of speech, and she laid her free hand on his chest. "A distraction. To forget if only for a moment." The pink tip of her tongue briefly touched her bottom lip, and lust shivered through his shaft. "You." It was pure glory to see that mouth form that one word. "Until I have the courage to tell you what you want to know... even though it has only been a handful of hours since we've met."

"Well, damn. It makes no sense."

"No, but then sometimes such things don't. There is only desire." Her shrug was slight. "Will you indulge me?"

How could he deny such a starkly honest request? "Hell, yes." It was merely the culmination of the teasing and tension exchanged between them since they'd met. He hooked his hand about her nape, dragged her to him, and then claimed her mouth with all the authority he'd wished to show the last time he kissed her.

The second Theodosia looped her arms about his shoulders and returned his kisses without shame or self-consciousness, he was lost. He wanted all of her, without barrier or excuse, but above that, he wished to treat her with care and respect, so she'd feel admired and desired, and he hoped she would feel protected, as if she weren't alone in this nightmare she'd landed in.

Over and over, he drank from her, tangled his tongue with hers as if there was only so much air left in the world and they two needed to share it. When that didn't prove enough contact, he walked her backward across the room and into the short corridor on the right side of the apartment that led to the bedchambers. When the wall prevented further movement, he hefted her upward with his hands hooked beneath her thighs, and as he pressed her into the wall, he renewed his efforts to kiss her senseless.

And she gave as good as she got. Was she merely desperate or did she truly want him? He rather liked to think it was the latter. Her fingers in the hair at his nape or tracing the scars on his cheek spurred him onward; the soft sounds of encouragement or pleasure she made in her throat enhanced his desire. With her ankles locked at the small of his back, they were layered together but there were entirely too many clothes between them.

"Hudson..." When she tugged on his hair, tiny pinpricks of pain skittered over his scalp and worked to further enhance the need hardening his shaft. "I want to see you, touch you," she whispered against his lips. "Taste you."

Oh, God.

"Ah, there's the woman who knows her own mind I glimpsed when we first met." Once more, he lifted her up, and since she kept her legs locked about his waist, he merely carried her into his room, crossed the room, and then set her on the edge of the four-poster bed. Damn but she looked all too delicious sitting there with her blonde hair escaping its pins, her skirts rucked up about her thighs and her legs naturally parted. "If you wish to beg off—"

"No." She curled the fingers of one hand into his cravat and brought him close. "This is just what I need right now. At least when I break, pleasure will accompany it and I won't feel… so horrid." Though her voice wavered on the last word, she surged upward, she claimed his mouth in such an enthusiastic kiss that her teeth grazed his lower lip.

White hot lust careened through his body, turning his blood into rivers of lava. This woman's overtures in the face of her fears and heartaches were the most erotic thing he'd ever experienced, and as his protective instincts welled, he acknowledged to himself that she'd perhaps burrowed beneath his skin when he'd not been looking.

Holding her head between his palms, he kissed her as if he had all the time in the world and alternately as if he didn't. Then the hold on his control slipped and he thought he might expire on the spot if he didn't see her body, if he wasn't given the chance to worship her as she ought to be. As he dragged his lips beneath her jaw with the intent to discover all her secrets, Hudson plucked the pins from her hair. The tiny *pings* as they hit the hardwood was the height of satisfying, especially when that blonde waterfall tumbled about her back and shoulders.

"Gorgeous." When she murmured something unintelligible, he kissed a path down her chest, traced the scoop of her bodice with his lips and fingertips. Hot skin tantalized, teased, as did her fingers as they worked the buttons of his jacket. In seconds, he'd encouraged the wine-colored garment from her frame. A piece of folded paper fluttered to the floor — no doubt the note that had caused her initial flight. He would pounce on that later. Pretending he hadn't seen it, when presented with her unmentionables, a certain hushed sacredness came over him as if he were gazing at a previously undiscovered work of art. "Ah, Theodosia."

"It has been a long time since I've seen such admiration, such desire, in a man's eyes." The throaty little laugh she uttered, the mischievous twinkle in her eyes, all worked at his undoing as she stood and pushed the jacket from his shoulders. "I have missed it, missed the being something to someone other than a mother." Her fingers were at the laces of his waistcoat while he worked the ones on her stays.

A tremble of need danced down his spine. "I well know what that feels like." Outside of this case, it seemed they had other things in common. Then the corset fell away, and it was one less barrier to seeing her naked glory.

"Mmm." She relieved him of the waistcoat. Setting to work on his cravat, she pressed heated kisses to the skin she uncovered from that length of fabric. The scrape of her teeth on his neck would send him into madness soon. "Too many clothes yet." That whisper held so much fervor, passion that he at once agreed.

Fabric fell to the floor in abandoned puddles. He toed off his boots, hopping, tugging the footwear from his person while she removed her petticoat. *Dear God*, in the afternoon sunlight the outline of her hardened, pink nipples was clearly visible. Quickly, he tugged the linen shirt from his body, and as she slowly removed that thin shift, he shucked out of his breeches. Arousal pulsed through his shaft; would she enjoy the sight of his erection, or would she shy away?

His ability to breathe completely left him, for she stood naked before him, and the air stalled in his lungs. She could have been a porcelain statue, except she was a living, breathing woman in his rooms, with round eyes full of need and her hands resting lightly on her rounded hips. From the swell of her modest breasts to the nip of her waist to the thatch of blonde curls at the apex of her thighs, she was every inch a goddess, descended from the heavens for his pleasure.

"Cat got your tongue?" The blatant look of invitation finally spurred him back to life.

Drawing in a breath, Hudson closed the distance. He slid a hand down her spine, brushed his fingers against the divot at the small of her back while she unashamedly explored the planes of his chest, his abdomen, glanced her fingertips along the curve of his backside. Every touch, each caress hurled him closer to the edge, but he didn't wish to waste time with words, so he kissed her, tangled his hands in her hair, tilted her head back, and kissed her as if that were his only purpose in life.

Theodosia sighed, put a palm to his cheek, swept it around to his nape and gently encouraged him closer with the veriest hint of pressure. She wriggled her hips into his, bumping his hardened member, and giggled when a hiss issued from him. "Well?"

"Vixen." He moved his hands to her waist; she was as fragile as the statue he'd likened her to, and when he tossed her onto the bed, her squeal of delight went straight to his stones. Perhaps he needed the distraction of her right now too. The case had been frustrating enough, and this would clear the air between them, shove the inappropriate thoughts from his mind so he could concentrate anew. "But damn if I'm not going to draw this out."

For them both.

In a twinkling, he joined her on the bed, but she wasn't having any of his domination — not yet. She pushed at his chest until he collapsed onto his back, looked at her as curiosity flowed through his veins. For the moment, he would let her have the upper hand. After, he would finish them both in hopefully spectacular fashion.

"You are even more interesting nude, Inspector." Theodosia straddled his knees, laid her palms on his hips with his erect shaft front and center.

He snorted in an effort to dislodge the desire that wanted to ignore foreplay. "I haven't been an inspector for years." When he reached for her, she batted his hands away. Clearly, she knew what she wanted and wouldn't be dissuaded.

"But that is what you are." Slowly, watching him the whole time, she leaned over. Strands of her hair tickled the sensitive skin of his member, and he sucked in a tight breath. "Except, for the next several minutes, you have my permission to abandon your duties and amuse yourself in many different ways." Then she pressed an open-mouthed kiss to his abdomen, dragged those lips up his chest. Her fingers followed, combing through the heavy mat of hair there, teasing the flat discs of his nipples with her nails until they grew erect, and another gasp escaped him.

He shivered from the erotic sensations and rather enjoyed her play. It wasn't often his bed partners came with such inventive torture, but even as she teased, there was an air of sadness and worry about her he wished to banish. At least for a little while. "Dia..." Where the shortened version of her name had come from, he couldn't say, but he rather like that too. It suited her.

"Hmm?" Dark desire and heat glimmered in the gray-blue pools of her eyes as she continued her exploration. "More, then?" Before he could comment, she once more leaned over him, her hair and nipples glancing over his skin, and when she closed her lips around the head of his straining length, he nearly vaulted off the bed.

"Ah!" His hips bucked, in an invitation or a simple reaction, he didn't know, but she merely chuckled and took him deeper into the warm cavern of her mouth, working him over as if they'd been together like this for an eternity. Fisting the bedding in his hands, he dug in his heels, tried to regulate his breathing, but she wasn't quite done with him.

She pulled off him, and with swollen lips, smiled. "Ready for the next course?"

"I... That depends." This was moving all too quickly, and he hadn't had enough time to explore her body, but that didn't seem to matter to her. Theodosia shifted position, came up his form to straddle his waist this time. "Let's put this nice, thick appendage to good use, hmm?"

"Wait, I—" His yelp changed into a groan as she slid easily upon his shaft, never stopping until he'd penetrated her fully. That heated sheath had his breath shuddering from his throat, and it was all he could do to grasp her hips and guide her movements. Was there ever a more beautiful sight than seeing a naked woman in all her glory as she rode atop her lover? "Damn."

"That might be high praise indeed, since you are a man of few words." She moved on him, taking him ever deeper with every gyration of her hips, every little wriggle and bounce, and there was a part of him that wanted nothing except to claim her, let her ride until they were both spent.

But that would mean this session was over all too soon. He wasn't ready to let her go yet. After a couple of thrusts into her honeyed heat, he couldn't survive the continued, sensual onslaught. "Enough." Tangling a hand in her hair, he pulled her down over his body in order to kiss her, show her in no uncertain terms he would guide this coupling, then his muscles tensed, and he flipped them both over. "My turn."

"Spoilsport." But she didn't bid him nay, even offered him a come-hither grin as their bodies came apart and the joining was broken.

"We shall see if you think so afterward." Settling between her splayed legs, Hudson spent the next several moments charting each and every one of her curves, learning the secrets of her body. When he strummed the pads of his thumbs over the hard tips of her nipples, the lady squirmed beneath him with a string of breathless moans. As he caressed a path between the perfect globes of her breasts and down to her navel, barely discernable gooseflesh popped on her skin. Laid out beneath him, he was both humbled and randy as he fondled and teased.

"Hudson... Please." She caught one of his hands and put it on her breast, clearly needing him there. "Send me over." For the first time since they'd met, there were no haunted shadows in her eyes.

"In a moment." Wishing to give them both maximum pleasure, he leaned over, kissed her lips then continued to kiss and nibble down her torso. The pebbled tip of a nipple against the flat of his tongue was everything he'd dreamed it might be, and the faint scent of lilacs as he licked his way over the soft swell of her belly drove him onward. Scooting down the mattress, he spread her thighs wider. "Ah, Dia. So lovely." Then he buried his head and finally tasted that inviting flesh, lapped at the moisture from their abbreviated joining, and their moans blended together.

"More." She furrowed her fingers into his hair, guided his head to where she wanted him, and those tiny pinpricks of pain enhanced his own need, pushed him ever closer to the edge. "Oh, yes!" Lost to the throes of pleasure as he worried that all-important little nubbin at her center, she clamped her knees to his ears and bucked her hips, putting her further at his mouth for greater devouring.

It took a concentrated suckle, a tickle of his tongue, the light scrape of his teeth to that tender piece of flesh to send her over the edge with a half-stifled scream and the wild bucking of her hips.

Pleased beyond measure and immensely aroused at how she'd pointed her toes as the release took her over, Hudson came back up her body, settled himself between her bent knees and then penetrated her, claimed her, speared into her heat until he was fully seated and irrevocably joined with her.

"Dear God." It was all too heavenly, a sort of unexpected welcome he hadn't had for far too long a time, and when he peered into her eyes, lost himself in those gray-blue pools, he came all too close to falling for her, of flying a little too close to her flame. "This... You..."

"Hush, Hudson. Concentrate on the matter at hand." The mix of censure and amusement in her voice proved too strong an aphrodisiac and prompted him into action.

Taking his weight onto one elbow, he clasped his other hand to her hip in a silent sign of possession, digging in his fingers, hoping he'd leave his mark, and then he began to move within her, and with each thrust into that welcoming, greedy heat, he fell down the rabbit hole into various possibilities.

Theodosia wrapped her arms about his shoulders, moved her hips in time to his strokes, and they soon fell into a pleasant, sweaty rhythm. Bodies crashed against each other, his heart pounded, her breath rasped in his ear. She encouraged him with moans and sighs. He answered her with the same, and through it all, he claimed her over and over, taking as much as she gave and reveling in the fact that this marvelous woman matched him in enthusiasm and stamina.

Tingles went through his stones which meant imminent release. When she nipped the side of his neck and squeezed her inner muscles to further tempt him, Hudson was lost. His strokes turned fast and frantic. She encouraged him with soft cries, and as she plucked at her nipple, that was the beginning of the end. Deeper, shorter, quicker his thrusting grew. As she cried out and her body stiffened and those inner walls fluttered with the first vestiges of release, he was hurtled into his own, and damn if he didn't come hard and intense as if he were a green boy just out of university.

Collapsing on top of her, he dragged breath into his lungs, buried his face into the crook of her shoulder as his heartbeat regulated and the world came back into order. "That was most satisfying."

"Yes, it was." The warmth of her breath skated across his cheek. "A wonderful distraction." She snuggled into him as she rolled onto his side and their physical connection was broken. "I knew you wouldn't disappoint with intercourse."

Heat went up the back of his neck. "Glad to be of service." Was that all she'd wanted him for? Had this coupling not meant as much to her as it had to him? Even accidentally?

Perhaps now was not the time to analyze… anything.

She lifted her head off his chest. "We should dress. There are things—"

"Shh. They can wait. Simply enjoy a few quiet moments." With a gentle hand to her head, he encouraged her back against him and then wrapped his arms about her. "There is plenty of time to resume our lives once this interlude is finished." Never had he wished to linger in a lover's bed, but with Theodosia, it felt right.

Reality would intrude soon enough.

Chapter Nine

Though she didn't wish to lose too much time by giving in to a nap, Theodosia reveled in the chance to recline in the former Bow Street Runner's embrace more than she probably should have. There was no shame in enjoying coupling with a man and the fact that she did prompted a faint smile. To say nothing of the fact that Mr. Ridley was quite proficient at it.

Nathaniel had been gone for over three years, and Hudson was the first man she'd trusted since she'd lost her husband. In his arms, she felt protected and safe, as if nothing bad could reach her, as if he alone could hold all the evil in the world at bay.

It was quite intoxicating, and she didn't want it to end.

Unfortunately, no matter how wonderful this interlude had been, this wasn't her reality. She was a widowed viscountess with a young son to raise and he was a former Bow Street inspector, retired in Rome with the intent to forget about his skills and talents. Eventually, she would need to return to England when Jacob was of an age to take up the reins of his father's title while Hudson would remain here in obscurity, to perhaps marry and have a family of his own. A life in which she was but a memory.

She must have made a sound of frustration or grief deep in her throat because he stirred and edged away only so much that he could peer into her eyes. "I hope you aren't regretting our time together."

That deep rumble of his baritone sent tickles into her chest. "Absolutely not." Not wanting the closeness between them to end, Theodosia pressed her lips to the underside of his jaw and rejoiced at the beginnings of stubble just coming to the surface. The contrast between the smooth skin of his neck and that rasp was highly addicting. "To be honest, I think we both needed this distraction."

"Indeed." He edged a hand down her back, following her spine to the curve of her rear. Shivers of renewed need followed in his wake. "You are tense again, which means your mind is once more on Jacob."

"Of course it is. I'm his mother." With a sick feeling in the pit of her belly, she pulled out of his arms and crawled to the side of the bed. "And because I have trusted you with the greatest intimacy, I now need to trust you with my greatest secret," she said in a choked whisper.

"Ah." Hudson planted an elbow on the mattress and put his head in his hand as he watched her move off the bed. "You speak of what you have been hiding, of what that letter referenced." It wasn't a question.

"Yes." Oh, he would certainly despise her once she told him, and that she couldn't bear, but there was nothing for it. "My husband and I kept the secret until his death, but now I cannot help wonder if that very secret isn't at the heart of this mess." Needing to put distance between them so he couldn't distract her with touches or caresses, Theodosia left the relative security of the bed. She padded around that massive piece of furniture, retrieved her abandoned shift, and then slipped it over her head.

All the while, he watched her with more than a trace of desire in those intense, ice blue eyes and a faint grin curving his mouth. He took in her every movement, and when his attention dropped to her breasts as she smoothed the fabric along her body, his regard tightened her nipples. "After what I have seen in my career as an investigator, anything is possible."

"I couldn't begin to imagine what you've seen." A shudder careened down her spine as she bent and snatched his breeches from the floor. Tossing them his way, she said, "Put these on."

"Why?"

"You are much too distracting like... that." Theodosia waved a hand at him to encompass his naked state, and that glorious appendage which had brought her to the heights of pleasure. Not that he hadn't done that with his lips and teeth...

With a chuckle, Hudson rolled off the bed. "Though I have much to say on the subject, I shall table it for the time being."

"Good." Of course she stared—ogled really—as he donned the article of clothing. How could she not? His large form commanded attention both fully dressed and not. That barrel chest and its mat of dark hair made her want to toss everything to explore it all the more. The narrowed waist, the faint lines of ridges at his abdomen, that thin ribbon of dark hair that led straight to his rather well-hung equipage that she wouldn't mind teasing again with her mouth... *Ah, drat.* He covered that interesting organ with the breeches. A sigh scudded from her throat as he manipulated the buttons of his frontfalls. At least it was hidden.

"Better?"

"Only just." There was still the matter of his bare chest, but she needed something to look at while she told her pathetic tale. With trepidation knotting through her belly, Theodosia retrieved the crumpled, folded note that had fallen from her bodice when he'd

undressed her. "This came from the Marquess of Hanneford. I had no idea he was in Rome; had no idea he even knew who I was... who Nathaniel was." Not able to read the horrid words of the letter again, she silently handed it to him.

"Thank you for the trust." As Hudson unfolded the paper and smoothed it out as best he could, Theodosia drifted toward one of the windows. The building heat would make the room stifling before too long, so she unlatched the catch and then pushed the glass open. Immediately, a gentle breeze came into the room, redolent of flowers and the scent of sun-heated stone.

"It wasn't given lightly." Still, she didn't turn around. Couldn't. To see censure or even pity in his eyes would break her.

For long moments, Hudson remained silent. How many times did he read the note? What were his initial impressions? She didn't know, but she gripped the window ledge so hard her knuckles showed white.

"Can I assume Jacob is not your real son?" Mild interest hung on the inquiry.

Swift pain went through her chest. "He is not." She forced moisture into her suddenly dry throat with a hard swallow. "While walking in Hyde Park one summer afternoon, Nathaniel and I stumbled upon a young maid who had just stowed a baby inside a bush."

"The devil you say!"

Only then did she turn and face him, but she didn't leave the relative safety of the window, had to keep the bed between them. "My husband detained the maid—who we then took into our own household. She is my lady's maid, Doris; I retrieved the babe. He couldn't have been more than a week old, but was clearly malnourished, dehydrated, and unwanted." A waver set up in her voice, and it took her some time to gain a modicum of control over her emotions. "After questioning the maid, finding out the baby was meant to be abandoned under orders, we brought him home."

"What happened then? Surely it was difficult to explain the sudden appearance of a baby." He crossed his arms at his bare chest, the letter still in hand.

"It was no secret Nathaniel and I had been trying for children, but since we were never blessed with offspring, this seemed the next best thing." She shrugged. There was no use in embellishing her history. "Thank goodness the cuts of women's clothing allow for generous folds that can hide—or display—one's figure depending on the look one wishes."

"So you pretended you were pregnant and then immediately went into false labor." It wasn't a question.

"Yes." She straightened her shoulders. "It was the least we could do, and afterward, we swore the household to secrecy regarding the pregnancy and birth under penalty of being let go without references. It was the only time I had the luxury of pretending I was with child, for fate was never kind to me in that way." For long moments, she looked at him, wondering what went through his mind from the tale. "After that, we were a happy family, just the three of us, and it was as if it had always been meant to be."

"Except the presence of your lady's maid had you recalling that day over and over."

"I couldn't leave Doris to the wolves either. Chances were high she would have been sacked anyway, from all the stories she'd told me over the years."

Hudson blew out a breath. Annoyance shadowed his face. "Who fathered Jacob?"

Fear climbed her spine and coldly twisted down her spine. "The Marquess of Hanneford." She pressed her trembling lips together, but at least the worst of the confession was done. "He fathered many bastards and there were rumors his young wife was increasing. However, she died suddenly, and everything was hushed. Some within the *ton* wondered if she died of natural causes, for Lord Hanneford has a temper. Did the babe die with her? I would imagine so, yet according to Doris, Jacob's birth mother was one of the marquess' many mistresses, who didn't want either of them."

His Adam's apple bobbed with a slow swallow. "Taking the babe—which didn't belong to you—is still a crime."

The urge to retch grew strong. "Perhaps so, but I gave that baby a new life, a *better* life. Hanneford could have sent him to an orphanage, but instead, he ordered him dumped in the park to die." She shook her head, took a few steps around the side of the bed. "I saved the boy. He's thriving and happy." Emotions plowed into her with the force of a blow. Tears gathered in her eyes. "So you tell me who committed the real crime, Mr. Ridley."

"Ah, so we are back to formalities, are we?" Low grade anger reverberated in his voice. Annoyance flashed in his eyes. By the second he grew more livid, for of course everything with the investigator was black and white.

"We are if you won't see my side of this."

"Hmph." He crumpled the note in his hand and then tossed it away. The paper ball rolled across the floor toward the door, where the cat then appropriated it and carried it somewhere else within the apartment. "Hanneford must have discovered that his by-blow wasn't dead and that his employee was missing." His frown was a fierce affair. "For whatever reason, the marquess must want the boy back, especially if Jacob looks like him. If things are desperate with fathering a child, it would stand to reason he'd want a rightful heir, perhaps even pass your son off as belonging to his wife."

"But Jacob is eight!"

"That matters not. Enough money offered, a few stories told into the right ears, a lie corroborated here and there, and suddenly, a missing heir is explained. The marquess comes back to England from being abroad, victorious, with his son. He is lauded a hero, and the line remains unbroken." The fact Hudson delivered this explanation with an impassive expression left her gasping and desolate. "Illegitimate sons have long been passed off as true heirs since time began."

"No!" Not having the strength to stand any longer, Theodosia collapsed into a nearby winged-back chair. The pile of books next to it slipped and crumpled to the floor with the veriest of whispers. "He is *my* son," she said before sobs overtook her. "*I* raised him. I *love* him." Why couldn't he understand this?

What the bloody hell?

She'd stolen a baby? The son she doted upon and paid him—Hudson—to locate after being kidnapped, had been taken by her in the first place?

Hudson struggled to contain his shock and annoyance. "You could have told me earlier." It sent the case careening into a different direction. Hell, there wasn't a case any longer.

"I know, but I was afraid, and there was no reason. We are in Rome. No one knows us here. If the marquess wanted his child, why didn't he try to take him back while I was in England?" Before he could answer, she launched onward, and he steeled himself against her tears. "Yes, I have made mistakes in my life. Perhaps taking that baby was one of them." The delicate tendons of her throat worked with a swallow. She clenched her hands tightly together in her lap. "But how could I, in good conscience, leave that little babe out in the elements to die because the damned marquess couldn't be bothered to look after his child—legitimate or otherwise?"

"That is not for me to answer." There were crimes of all sorts that people perpetrated in this world, and from his way of thinking, a sin was a sin. Why should he overlook her breaking the law when he prosecuted others?

"Don't you see?" She implored him with luminous eyes and moisture-spiked lashes, her chin quivering. "Hanneford is *not* a good man."

Every part of him balked against her story, and for years he'd trained himself not to get involved in the personal lives of either the victims or their families. As best he could, Hudson hardened his heart; he had a job to do.

"That doesn't matter. What you did was a crime. You stole a child." It still boggled his mind, but then, she had a compassionate heart. Hadn't he already seen evidence of that?

She scrubbed at the tears on her cheeks. Fire flashed deep in her eyes. Oh, she was well and truly displeased with him. "Then arrest me, Hudson. Take me back to England and into Whitehall."

"I can't—"

But she wasn't done. "Lock me away for being a good person, for caring, for giving that boy a home, for wanting to be a mother so badly my maternal instincts and protection welled when I saw him in that bush." More tears fell and she pushed out of the chair. "I am proud of what I did, what Nathanial and I did. No one deserved to be parents more than us, and now…" Her voice broke and she put a hand to her cheek. She swayed where she stood. "And now, that compassion, that one tiny decision has led to this!"

Apparently, he was only so strong. His chest tightened at her distress. "Please stop."

She sliced a hand through the air in frustration. "You are the one who is making me feel like a criminal when you should be hunting down the people the marquess has probably employed. He stole my son. He kidnapped the boy, and no matter what you say, I want Jacob back."

For the first time in his life as a retrieval expert, he'd crossed the line into confusion and doubt. Could it be his beliefs, his ideals on how to describe crime were wrong? But her words stung, especially after what they'd just shared. "You think to criticize my methods when you have complicated this whole thing due to not being fully truthful with me from the start?"

"One would think that a man of your reputation could have worked around that missing information." Again, she swayed, and he silently cursed.

At the situation. At her for withholding. At himself for being perceived as an arse. Looking at the case from her perspective, nurturing such a large secret for the last eight years couldn't have been easy. His insistence on protocol wavered as compassion and protection welled to obliterate everything else. A long-suffering sigh escaped him, and he was all too aware of the open window and the possibility they might be overheard. "I don't want to fight, Dia." Again, he used the shortened version of her name, and when her chin trembled, some of his reserve crumbled. "I don't want to sully what we shared." A muscle twitched in his cheek, and he reminded himself to unclench his jaw. "But you have to know withholding this information has skewed my investigation. Had I been apprised of the marquess' possible involvement, I could have discovered he was in Rome yesterday."

"I know." A sob followed and she peeled herself out of the chair. "I didn't know what to do because I can see how much you despise my decisions." As she tried to skirt around him, Hudson's reserve broke all the way down.

"Wait." The poor thing. She truly wasn't one of those women who cried prettily. Oh, no. Theodosia's face was mottled red, her nose was running, and there were strands of damp hair stuck to her cheeks. "I'm sorry." With a sigh, he moved close, wrapped her in an embrace he hoped would make her feel safe, and held her close. "I have been alone far too long and don't remember how to be around people without acting gruff and an arse." That wasn't something to be found at the bottom of a bottle of brandy.

"I deserve the chastisement." When she rested her head on his chest, the moisture from her tears wet his skin. He rather liked that bit of intimacy which was very different than bedding her. "I apologize as well." She sniffled. "I should have been truthful with you from the start, but I couldn't put my son at further risk. And now he just might be."

Not knowing how to comfort her, Hudson guided her to the chair, and when he dropped into it, he settled her into his lap with her legs hanging off one of the arms. He continued to hold her close. "One problem at a time, hmm?" For the space of a few heartbeats, silence reigned. Then he pressed his lips to the top of her head. "I have always been honest with you, haven't I?"

"Yes." The word was small and was lost into the noise of the afternoon outside the window.

Up and down, he stroked a hand on her back in the attempt to soothe. "This delay *might* have put him further in jeopardy this is true. However," he said when she stiffened, "If the marquess indeed needs him as an heir, the boy would be well cared for. Under guard, of course, but not in imminent danger. I am not about to give up."

Theodosia pulled slightly away and peered upward into his face. "You will help retrieve him for me?"

"Yes, and from everything you've told me about the boy, he is kind and sensitive and clever—like his mother. His *real* mother." With a tight chest, he gently wiped at the tears that lingered on her cheeks. It was such a trusting, intimate act, and he realized he wanted more of than in his life. "Such a remarkable boy doesn't deserve what's happened to him. I want to see him safe at home—with you."

Despite the crime she had committed.

Despite the laws she'd broken.

Despite it going against his sense of duty.

"Oh, Hudson!" Then her arms were about his shoulders. She pulled his head down and soundly kissed him. There was a bit of frantic emotion in that embrace that only served to reignite his desire. Did it have the same effect on her?

The more he attempted to fight that reaction, the more he ended up on the losing side of that internal war. This vulnerable, determined woman had crept into his life had had begun to lay siege to his heart without his knowing or his permission, and he so much wanted to cry defeat and kneel before her. He was done with his ordinary, dull, retired life.

So he did what any man would do. He kissed her back, claimed her mouth with matching fervor until his length shuddered to life and fires once more licked through his veins. What did it say about him that he was essentially agreeing to blur the lines between black and white merely because of a pretty face and a handful of tears? But it was more than that. Her tale was as heartfelt as any he'd heard, and what she'd said did have merit and had rung with a grain of truth.

You're getting soft, Ridley.

He grinned against her lips and then helped her to resettle into his hold by straddling his lap. Perhaps that wasn't such a bad thing. If one little change in decision could make her so very happy, where was the harm? They could meet the next handful of challenges as they came — together.

What an odd feeling, and even more strangely, he welcomed it.

Chapter Ten

As much as Theodosia secretly wanted another go 'round in bed with Hudson, she had to content herself with several moments of lovely kissing before leaving his lap to begin dressing.

Perhaps there would be time for such scandal later. For now, Jacob was still missing, and they needed to devise a plan to retrieve him. Yet she couldn't release the feelings of restlessness that assailed her. What she required was another distraction even if sharing the greatest intimacy had left her oddly free and liberated in a way.

Surely indulging in intercourse wasn't the only reason for those surprising emotions.

Not having the answers, she continued to dress in silence. He'd assisted her with the stays, and she'd done the same with his waistcoat. The cotton of her wine-colored dress was hopelessly wrinkled, and anyone with half a brain would know what she'd been doing, but there was nothing for that now.

After using the commode in the water closet attached to the bedroom—what a novel idea and invention!—which was a pretty wooden cabinet over a chamber pot, she freshened up in the water basin in a matching wooden wash stand also in the cozy room. A quick peek into a partially clouded mirror above helped her to pin her hair into some semblance of respectability. Once she presented herself to him and finding him in his shirtsleeves rolled up to the elbows, she stifled a sigh.

Truly, it was criminal the man was so attractive no matter what he wore… or didn't.

He glanced at her with the same intensity he always had, but his emotions didn't show through to his expression. "In my fervor earlier, I wasn't in my right mind, should have donned a sheath, so I—"

Well, drat. "Stop." Theodosia held up a hand as her chest tightened. "As I mentioned in the conversation that followed our… time together," she forced a hard swallow into her suddenly dry throat, "I mentioned that I never found myself with child, so clearly, that isn't something my body is capable of." Though her voice wavered, she overlooked it. "There is no need to worry that consequences will disrupt your life."

"Ah." It was too difficult to ascertain if that flicker of something in his eyes was disappointment or pity. "You have already endured so much in your life, that you were perfectly justified in your determination to find Jacob."

"Yes." When her chin trembled, she wished the floor would open up and swallow her whole. "Nathaniel and I saw various midwives. All of them agreed 'something wasn't quite right' with my womb, and that though a pregnancy wasn't impossible, it would be very, very difficult to achieve."

For long moments, Hudson remained quiet, and she died a thousand deaths to know the thoughts in his head. Would that sour him on the chance they might have a relationship together after this current case had concluded? Then, he nodded. "I haven't seen you with Jacob, but I suspect you are a wonderful mother and one he dotes upon." He raised a hand, perhaps to touch her, cup her cheek, but then apparently changed his mind and let it drop to his side. "You have far too much to give the world that goes beyond motherhood. Please don't pin your worth on just that."

"Oh." Her chin trembled. Sometimes, what he said surprised her and rocked the foundations of her heart. "Thank you. I... I appreciate that. In recent weeks, I have realized that for myself and want to discover who I am in the world."

"Good." Confusion lined his face before resolve took over. "I should escort you home."

"I'm not ready." She frowned, for her brother would soon be home, and she didn't wish to face questions or lectures. Heat seeped into her cheeks. "This, uh, jaunt to your rooms has been exactly what I needed—both physically and emotionally." Remarkably, she was better able to see the investigation through. "I'm glad for the confession, frankly."

"I am glad you told me as well, but perhaps for different reasons." He followed her progress across the floor to the window. "If you refuse to go home, where, then? And do you wish for company?"

Oh, he was so dear with that trace of vulnerability! "The Trevi fountain. It's one of Jacob's favorite spots in the city. Perhaps he was allowed to go, and it's early yet. Just after teatime at that." The afternoon was lovely, and echoes of children somewhere nearby toyed with her heart. "There might be a chance…"

"I realize you are anxious for a glimpse of him, but the likelihood Jacob will be there…" She must have made a soft sound of distress, for he joined her at the window and laid a gentle hand on her shoulder. "You shouldn't torture yourself merely for the hell of it. No matter what happens, you will need to dig into your hidden strength."

Though the words weren't necessarily ones of comfort, they indeed had her straightening her spine. She craved more of his warmth, more of that connection than merely a hand on a shoulder, but perhaps that was madness, for it had only been one day since they'd met. "I need to do this, Hudson. Even if there is a remote possibility of seeing him, of perhaps snatching him back, I must." Turning to face him, she peered up into his face, traced her fingertips along the side of his face where the shadow of stubble was just beginning to form. "Can you not understand that?"

He clasped her fingers, brought them to his lips. "I do, of course, but I want you to prepare yourself for every eventuality."

"I know." It was so tempting, his proximity, the rich timbre of his voice, the want of burrowing into his arms and letting him keep the world at bay, but she had already had her distraction; there wasn't time for another. "Once I see for myself—good or bad—I will then go home. Perhaps I will rest, but how can I when Jacob's future is uncertain? When every thread of goodness I have wrapped him in is on the verge of unraveling?"

It was a terrible burden to bear, this being a mother, and one she'd had no idea the full scope of when she'd plucked her son from that bush in Hyde Park so long ago. But she wouldn't have it any other way.

"You will put one foot in front of the other and meet each minute, each hour, as they come until we can bring him home." The emotions in his eyes were impossible to read, but when he moved his fingers to rest lightly beneath her chin and he claimed her lips in a barely there kiss, a shudder of *something* danced down her spine. "Come. While we are out, we shall have a bit of dinner. Ingesting only tea will not sustain us through the night."

"Perhaps." With a hint of a smile, she pushed around him in search of her slippers. "Let us hope we can slip past your landlady without incident." The last thing she needed was knowing glances and to be beset with matchmaking plans.

Since the weather was quite lovely, there was a fair amount of people visiting the piazza di Trevi. Tourists and locals alike milled about the Palazzo Poli. Tantalizing scents of tomato and spices filled the air from vendors selling their mouth-watering treats from handcarts. Others sold various sweets, and there were always happy customers willing to put forth a coin or two to tease their tastebuds.

Once Theodosia alighted from a hired carriage and accepted Hudson's crooked arm, she sent her glance about the immediate area in the search of her son. Through the crowd of laughing, happily chattering people, she didn't see a familiar little suit or the head of blond hair she'd ruffled and kissed for so many years.

"Let us stroll for a bit, to do some proper surveillance, and then perhaps you can wade into the fountain." A hint of humor danced in his voice as he set them into motion.

"How did you know I wished to at least put my feet in the water?"

When he shrugged, his shoulder brushed hers and tiny frissons of electric need went through her. "I didn't, but knowing how much you enjoy this area, I made a guess." A grin curved his lips. "Truth be told, I wouldn't mind that either. The heat lingers into the evening, and it is only May."

"Even if bathing is frowned upon by the polizia if they are in the area?" Would this be another instance of him crying law breaker and her defending the decision?

He waggled his bushy eyebrows. "They cannot decry what they don't see."

Was he flirting with her? How lovely. "Take heed, Mr. Ridley. I might be corrupting you." Then she winked. "But perhaps the reason for that is over stimulation this afternoon." Was it really her flirting back with such a smokiness in her voice? When the rumble of his laughter erupted into the air, she couldn't help a smile. Though circumstances were drastic, a bit of humor and banter went long ways into surviving it.

"Ah, that might be the reason indeed." The scars pulled at his cheek with his grin and recalled the fact he hadn't yet shared how he'd come by the injuries. "It is not every day an ordinary man such as me is hired by a beautiful viscountess. Let alone picked to do other… things with."

She snorted as they wove between the many people in the crowd. "I rather think I'm ordinary as well." Slightly, Theodosia tightened her fingers on his arm. "By the by, I was called a Diamond of the First Water in my Come Out. There were wagers on which bachelor I would choose to marry in the betting book at White's, on who would win me."

"Did Nathaniel's name enter into any of those wagers?"

A giggle escaped. "Absolutely not. No one took him seriously, for he wasn't as dashing as others, and he certainly hadn't the fortune of a few." She winked at him. "That is what I liked about him, though. He wasn't like all the other men of the *ton*."

Neither was the man at her side, but was there enough between them for a future beyond this case? Or had he spent too much time alone and wasn't looking for fetters? Then she mentally gave her head a shake. Was marriage even what he wanted for herself? Everything would depend on what happened with Jacob.

"I can understand that about you." He nudged her ribs with his elbow. "But I can also see what my own eyes tell me. You are beautiful, and I don't accept arguments."

"Pish posh." Yet pleasure warmed her chest, nonetheless. After they'd done a circuit of the area — without noting a glimpse of her son — and arrived at the lip of the fountain, she tossed what she hoped was a playful glance over her shoulder at him. "Are you keen to get wet, Mr. Ridley?"

Shock jumped into his expression, and then his eyes darkened as he looked at her. "I can't think of anything I would enjoy more right now, Lady Ballantyne," he managed in a choked whisper.

Only then did she realize the unintended double entendre. Heat slapped at her cheeks as she toed off her slippers. "I..." Since no one about them paid the slightest heed, she let the slippers drop to the cobblestones and then hefted the bulk of her skirting with one hand. "Just for a few minutes." With a giggle, Theodosia clambered over the low stone lip and once her feet and calves were in the cool water, a sigh escaped. "Oh, that is refreshing."

"Damn." The investigator plopped himself onto the fountain's lip, removed his boots and socks, left them where they fell, and then joined her in the water.

The sight of his bared calves with the sprinkling of dark hair temporarily rendered her speechless. Was there anything more glorious than spying various bits of a man's form scandalously uncovered from beneath proper clothing? Could she encourage him to remove the jacket so she could once more see him in his shirtsleeves?

Get hold of yourself, Theo. This is naught but a temporary bit of insanity to help you through a hardship.

"You still look overheated." Feeling oddly lighthearted if still concerned, she put a hand into the water and flung the cool liquid in his direction.

A growl emanated from him. "Turnabout is fair play, my lady." He scooped up water for himself and splashed it in her direction.

She squealed in mock-outrage. A few minutes were spent acting like children as they sought to douse each other with a bit of water. Afterward, when her gown was hopelessly spotted and his cravat was damply limp and droplets glimmered in his dark hair, they amused themselves by wading in the water.

Once, when she caught him in a laugh, she smiled at him, and their gazes met.

Companionship and something much more than that was exchanged between them. It was stupid and silly, but it couldn't be ignored. She was developing feelings for this man. The knowledge stunned her, sent shock through her chest and flutters into her belly. Possibly inconceivable, of course, after only a handful of hours, but there was no explaining what fate did.

And she had forgotten how lovely such feelings were.

Movement out of the corner of her eye jogged her attention and when she turned her head to see what triggered her notice, a gasp whooshed from her throat. "Dear God." Forgetting for a moment she was in a pool of water, she clung to Hudson's strong arm with both hands. The hem of her gown would inevitably be soaked but there was nothing for it.

"What is it?" Immediately on guard, he put a hand to the small of her back and shielded her body from the direction in which she looked.

"Him. The Marquess of Hanneford is *here*." Fear twisted down her spine and went back up to fight with a strong push of anger. As she tugged Hudson around, panic welled in her chest. No matter how much she strained to see, she didn't see her son. "Jacob is not."

"Remain calm, Dia." His use of the unusual nickname brought a trace of tears to her eyes. "Let us exit the fountain but don't draw attention to ourselves. If he's not alerted to your presence, he won't run or cause a scene."

She nodded, not trusting her voice, and allowed him to help her out of the water. Without comment, she jammed her slippers onto her feet while he struggled into his socks and boots. It didn't matter her stockings were hopelessly soaked. Every second that passed, her heartbeat tripped faster. Darkness crept around the edges of her vision.

"Tell yourself that you will not faint in public," he whispered into her ear as he leaned over her, made certain she was comfortable sitting on the fountain's lip. "Stay here. I am going to reconnoiter then I'll come report back."

"But…" She clung to his hand even as the crowds surged and cavorted around them.

Hudson met her gaze. "I promise to come back. We must know the enemy before we can confront him, and this is what you sought me out to do." With a squeeze of her fingers, he slipped away, and all too soon melted into the crush.

Minutes passed. Restless energy propelled her off the fountain's lip. Keeping to the more crowded patches filling the piazza, she crept ever closer to where she'd last seen the marquess. He stood amidst a group of other English, French, and Italian society people; one of them looked like a local official with various medals jingling on a light blue uniform jacket.

The pleasing sound of accented voices fell to her ears. When Hanneford said something, polite laughter went through the knot around him.

Oh, the gall of him! To have taken her son and stowed him away so he could do the pretty with these people. She wanted to rail at him, claw at his eyes, demand that he tell her where Jacob was, but she couldn't for it might jeopardize the boy's life and call attention to her own. Men like Hanneford would undoubtedly have paid people to remain on his side regardless of how foul he was. She couldn't help Jacob if she were tossed into a Roman prison.

"I thought I told you to stay put?" The whisper in her ear carried a hint of annoyance with it as Hudson slipped an arm about her shoulders and urged her away from her quarry. "If he had seen you, made a fuss, ordered your arrest…"

That hint of panic in his tones fired her own. "I apologize, but I couldn't sit there and do nothing. I had to see for myself."

"I understand, truly I do, and yet you will draw attention to yourself with that wet hem until it dries." He drew her to the opposite side of the piazza and then down a shallow alley until they reached an outdoor trattoria where the most appetizing, savory aromas filled the air. "However, you must be careful. It's a sticky wicket we're in to be sure, and part of my duty to this case is keeping you safe."

"While I appreciate that, when it comes to my son, I am a bit crazed."

"No, my lady. Determined. You are determined."

"Perhaps." She frowned as he ushered her into a wooden chair at one of the small, round tables. "What have you discovered?"

"Hanneford will attend a dinner party thrown by the man with the medals on his chest. They had come to visit the fountain beforehand, for his villa isn't far from here."

"And yet we waste time to eat ourselves." It was unreasonable to be cross with him; it wasn't Hudson's fault the marquess had made an appearance. Fear twisted down her spine. "We cannot let him leave Rome with my son." Her voice broke on the last word, but her companion didn't answer straightaway, for a footman arrived at their table. She waited in silence as Hudson gave him an order for dinner, and only once the man took himself off again, did the investigator grin.

"Nourishment is essential for what is coming next."

Unexpected flutters went through her belly. "Meaning?"

"You and I are going to monitor the property where he is set to go, and with any luck, they will all dine alfresco, or the dining room windows will be thrown open to catch the evening breeze." He winked. "I am not above skulking in shrubberies for good information."

"There are times when I am in awe of you, Mr. Ridley." Though she used his formal title since they were in public, she would rather have called him by an endearment, and that hadn't been her wont in a very long time indeed.

What is happening to me?

"Then prepare to be amazed, Lady Ballantyne, for I have ordered us one of the tastiest dishes—and my favorite—in all of Rome for our dinner." Dear heavens, when he grinned at her like that, years fell from his face and his eyes twinkled with deviltry. How had she ever thought him plain?

"Oh?"

"Indeed." He settled into his own chair and rested his large hands loosely on the tabletop. "*Cacio e Pepe* made with fresh egg tonnarelli is one of this region's oldest dishes, as well as quite simple. Peasant food, if you will."

"It sounds amazing." Though, anything would in that baritone she could listen to him for hours.

"I stumbled upon it shortly after I came to Rome, and for the first two weeks here, after I secured lodging, I studied the people of the Eternal City through the food they enjoyed. This dish uses aged pecorino sheep cheese and lashings of black pepper."

"That is all? But how can that be?" Truly, she felt a dunce in front of him, this man who held knowledge in his brain that surpassed any titled aristocrat who'd gone to university or tarried in the hallowed halls of gentleman's clubs in London.

It was quite intoxicating, that intelligence.

Hudson's eyes twinkled. "According to tradition, shepherds carried these non-perishable ingredients with them on their arduous journeys deep into the Lazio countryside with their flocks. You see, sheep's cheese was the only ingredient they could reliably call upon, and something they could come by easily enough. When hunger hit in the wilderness, the humble herdsmen cooked up the pasta on a campfire, mixed in the cheese and black pepper and then had a lovely, filling meal that barely touched the coin in their pouches."

By the time he'd finished telling the story, two bowls of the simple Roman dish had arrived at their table, along with two glasses of deep, red wine. The sharp aromas from the cheese and pepper teased Theodosia's nose, and her stomach grumbled.

"It smells divine."

"Tastes even better," he said as he snapped open his linen napkin with verve.

"Thank you, Hudson." Her voice wavered as she once more eyed him. "For everything you have done today already, for what you will do tonight."

A red flush rose over his collar. "It is truly my pleasure."

And I suspect that you are mine. She forced a hard swallow into her throat. Finally, it felt as if they were close to getting Jacob back. Aloud, she said, "I look forward to continuing the chase." Did she mean him pursuing her or of them tracking down Jacob?

Why not both?

Chapter Eleven

With his belly full, and his spirit satisfied for the first time in far too long, Hudson couldn't help a grin as he and Theodosia strolled along a private street lined with a high wall draped with pink and white bougainvillea. The sun would set soon and provide them with much-needed obscurity, but for the time being, he needed to find a way onto the property before they could look for a hiding place.

"I always wondered why it must be like to attend one of those fancy parties the rich nobs throw in Mayfair." His chuckle held a self-conscious air as they walked side by side. "No offense meant for present company, of course."

The sound of her giggle went straight to his stones. "I take no offense." When her arm brushed his, awareness shuddered down his spine. "Quite frankly, most of those events are the height of dull." Mischief sparkled in her eyes, and in the nearly golden light, she could have been a goddess who stepped right off a pedestal in a temple. "I am not particularly fond of stodgy old dinner parties or the relentless flirting of men who only want a wife who brings with her contracts that further his holdings." Her tentative grin faltered. "Then will go back to their mistresses once the newness of the union wears off."

"Except with the incomparable Nathaniel." Talking with this woman was both comforting and exciting. Her trials and struggles made him think that all of his had been worth it, and truth be told, he was a tiny bit jealous of the dead viscount, for he'd had years with Dia, years of laughter, and sadness, and loving.

"Yes, well, he *was* exceptional," she agreed in a soft voice, "but not incomparable." Sadness clouded her eyes, gone with her next blink. "There are many men such as him who are compassionate, humble, honorable, kind... attractive." Briefly, she held her bottom lip between her teeth, and he couldn't help staring at her mouth.

"Do you include me in that mix?" How, exactly, did she think of him?

"I do, but I would also add two more descriptors for you."

"Oh?" He paused at a part of the wall shaded by a few fruit trees. This section was near the end of an alley where people would seldom pass.

"Yes." She paused beneath one of the trees with a hand to its trunk, looking for all the world like a tourist lost on an unfamiliar, unmarked street, especially with her watermarked hem. "Grounded and tenacious. At times stubborn or a touch judgmental would be a better descriptor, but that makes you all the more interesting."

He chuckled and didn't even mind her assessment. "That's three words."

"So it is." Theodosia's hand brushed his. "I never was proficient at mathematics."

All too easily could he see himself falling for her, perhaps he already was, but it made no sense. Love didn't happen in a matter of hours. He stifled a snort of derision. Neither did blinding passion that made him take a woman he hardly knew to bed merely because she asked, because there was an inexplicable connection between them.

What would Mrs. Claudian say about that?

"I believe you know more than you assume, and that in extreme circumstances, your strength and abilities will set tongues wagging with amazement."

"Do hush." The blush on her cheeks might have been from the sun but he rather thought it was from his flirting. When her rosy lips parted slightly and a come-hither look appeared in her eyes, he very nearly kissed her right there in public where anyone could come upon them even if they were alone at the moment. Then she came to her senses. "Why are we here when we can gain access to the grounds by way of the drive?"

"We could, but I thought it might be more fun to go over the wall." Being in Theodosia's company made him feel reckless and young again, gave him a renewed purpose in life. Not once today had he wanted a drink. "What do you say? Do you wish for an adventure? Just imagine the tale you'll have to tell Jacob."

Joy passed over her face. "What a wonderful idea!" She sidled closer. "What do we do?"

"Well, first I'll lift you up the wall. While you are perching on the top, I'll climb up, drop to the ground, and then catch you as you push off." So saying, he bent and formed a loop with his hands. "Foot in here and then I'll boost you."

Once she hiked up her skirts, Theodosia laid her hands on his shoulders, fit her right foot into his cupped hands, and squealed with either delight or dismay when he stood and lifted her upward until she scrambled onto the lip of the ten-foot wall.

"Now wait there and I'll…"

With a hoot of exhilaration, the foolish woman launched herself from the wall and landed with an "oomph" onto the ground. "Ouch." It was followed by a giggle then a groan that made his chest seize. "I'm down. Slightly hurt but well."

Apparently, she'd taken to adventure with eyes wide open. He stifled a sigh, shook his head, and then hooked a booted foot into a vee of one of the trees. From there, he jumped, grabbed hold of the wall's lip, and pulled himself to the top. As soon as he swung a leg over to the other side, he glanced downward to spy Theodosia sitting on the grass inspecting her ankle. "Coming down," he called softly. Seconds later, he slid silently to the ground, using the wall as support so he wouldn't tumble as she had.

The back part of the property was comprised of manicured gardens with walking paths that winded through ornamental shrubberies, fruit trees, olive trees, flower beds and the like. The floral scents and the smells of growing things assailed his nose as he moved to her location and kneeled before her.

"Can you walk?" He took her ankle in hand, gently turned her foot this way and that as he inspected it.

"I hope so." Dirt and grass stained the skirt of her gown. There was a tiny tear near one of the short sleeves. A faint smear of dirt marred one cheek. "I was a bit enthusiastic."

"Yes, you were." And it had been fantastic if terrifying. As he spoke, he slipped his gloved hands along her ankle, then feeling a bit wicked, Hudson caressed further north to encompass her shapely calf. "Any pain?" He certainly didn't have any. In fact, one particular portion of his anatomy was very interested in investigating deeper beneath her skirting.

"Not that is bothersome." The words were soft, breathless as she looked at him from beneath her bonnet and behind the relative privacy behind the shrubberies. "Though I haven't tested bearing weight on it."

He continued his exploration, and damn if he didn't wish he'd left the gloves behind so he could feel her skin. "We can't be too careful, hmm?"

"No..." Her limb trembled while he drew his fingers up and down her lower leg. "Good thing you are so attentive."

Apparently, he was incapable of not being near her let alone touching her. "Truly, we should probably have you stand." Later, perhaps, he could play between her legs.

"I suppose." Her eyes had darkened either from reaction or his touch he couldn't say, but it was all too heady to wonder about. "Though this is lovely..."

"Agreed." With reluctance, Hudson scrambled to his feet then offered a hand to her. When she slipped her fingers into his palm, he hefted her into an upright position. "Test the ankle's strength."

With a small huff of apparent frustration, she did as he asked. "There is nothing but an initial twinge. I will be able to walk."

The annoyance tugged a grin from him. She was adorable at times. "I'll make it worth your while." When she didn't appear convinced, he pulled her close and stole a quick kiss. "Come, my lady. Let us discover whether our quarry is inside or outside."

"Fine." She was a bit mollified about the kiss, but clearly, she was still frustrated.

As was he. What was it about this woman that made him wish to hole up in his rooms with her in his bed without leaving for days on end for both love making and conversation?

They stuck to the walking gardens. As the sun began its descent, they reached the end, and not ten feet from the high shrubberies that shielded them was a long table set with elaborate decorations, cloth, and china. Silverware and silver serving trays glinted in the golden light. The soft clink of crystal against crystal rang in the air. Above everything, the buzz of conversation reached his ears, quite clearly in fact.

"Shit. They decided to dine outside after all," he said in a barely audible whisper. He looked askance at her. "My apologies for the vulgarity."

"Pish posh. It's rather exhilarating." She glanced at him with round eyes. "What now?"

He crept as close as he could and then tugged her down amidst the shrubbery, trees, and bushes. "Sit or lounge here with me. We can shamelessly listen to their conversation and perhaps glean what Hanneford's next plans are. If we're lucky, perhaps we can find an opening in which will allow us to retrieve your son."

"We might as well, since we both look like a dog's breakfast by now." Much to his surprise, she relaxed enough to lounge back on the grass and gazed at him with her gray-blue eyes full of expectation. "How scandalous."

"You *do* seem properly horrified about it," he couldn't help but tease as he settled on his side with an elbow in the grass and his head propped in his hand. Unlike other women of his acquaintance, being with Theodosia was all too easy. She made him feel as if his appearance didn't matter, as if his mistakes in the past didn't either.

"Properly," she said on the heels of a poorly stifled giggle. Amusement danced in her eyes. "Do you truly think they'll discuss anything of import?"

"Who knows, but it will be interesting to listen." He strained his ears and then sighed. "Unfortunately, all those pompous arses are only trying to impress each other with the tales of things I'll wager they've never done, seen, or experienced."

"Isn't that what most men do?" Leaning back on her elbows, she lifted her chin and smiled into the golden sky where a few wispy clouds floated across as the sun continued to set.

"Only the bad ones." Ah, she made quite the picture, and it was all he could do to remain sedately at her side instead of take her into his arms in a stranger's garden. "Men like me, men like your Nathaniel, we are men of action and experience. We would rather do for ourselves than have someone do for us."

"That is what sets you apart." The look in her eyes had awareness washing over him. Then her gaze jogged to the side of his face. "In the spirit of all that, tell me how you acquired the scars. It is no doubt an exciting story."

It had finally come to this, then. He would need to let down every one of his guards and indulge her, tell her of his darkest and weakest moments, which would make him vulnerable, possibly pathetic in her eyes.

"I suppose you will badger me until I do, hmm?"

"It's only polite, since you seem to have quite the knack for pulling secrets from me," she rejoined in a whisper.

"Fine." He once more listened to the dinner conversation to assure himself the guests still blathered on about inconsequential things. "But please know I don't share this because I want sympathy. Neither do I want your pity."

She resettled onto her side to face him. "As if I would do that." When she briefly rested a hand on his chest, he swallowed audibly. "You didn't treat me with the same at my heartfelt revelation."

"No, but I didn't give you the benefit of the doubt, either." Yet it had been this woman who'd prodded him to change his thinking.

"You didn't arrogantly cling to your opinion, though. *That's* what counts." One of her blonde eyebrows rose. "Let's have it, then."

Dogged determination, that's what she was made up just now. Charming, simply charming. "It all started two and a half years ago. At the time, I was a principal officer with Bow Street, on track to be made inspector and have my own team."

"Impressive."

"It was, and perhaps that went to my head. I don't know." Hudson frowned as he pondered carefully his next words. "The scars were gained during my last case—the greatest challenge of my career. One that I thought would win me that promotion."

"Yet, it obviously didn't because you are here, and if you hadn't been, I would never have met you or subsequently hired you," she reminded him in a low voice.

A simple quirk of fate that had completely upended his life.

He gave her a nod then listened once more to the dinner party conversation. The subject had shifted to matters of a political nature. "In any event, I had the misfortune of working the latest case of a serial killer—with more than a few horrid inclinations running especially toward women and children. He'd strangled and then cut open a young woman's guts, leaving her innards flung across a London street. It had the earmarks of four other murders, but this time, we had amassed enough clues to ascertain this man's identity."

Shock flickered through Theodosia's expression. "Good Lord. What you must have seen." One of her hands crept to her throat.

"I will spare you the worst." Some of his stories weren't fit for genteel ears. "One night, while in pursuit of my quarry, I was ambushed by a different criminal entirely." Telling her the story in a whisper added thrill to it.

"Not a related case?"

"No. Merely sheer dumb luck, as the Americans say." He shrugged, kept his voice low. "The places in London where I happened to investigate are not the sort of neighborhoods that host garden parties and routs."

She shivered and then squirmed into a sitting position with her legs folded beneath her. "Go on."

"Well, after a bit of a tussle wherein we exchanged punches, my opponent pulled out a knife with a wickedly serrated blade." His voice hitched, for he'd only told the story a few times since the injury. "That night it was dark and raining. I couldn't see clearly, especially with one of my eyes swollen shut due to a blow. By the time the blade flashed, there was no time to avoid it."

"Oh, no." Her eyes were round and rivetted on his face.

"The man lashed out, and though I did my best to defend and sidestep the attack, that blade carved up my left cheek and temple." He let his gloved fingertips drift over the mangled, puckered skin. "I'd never known such pain until my face was sliced open. The cuts went deep, obviously. I couldn't stop to do anything about it, for I went after the knife-wielding man—"

"With a vengeance, no doubt."

"Indeed." The corners of his lips twitched with a grin. "Eventually, after another round of fisticuffs, I left him incapacitated enough to bind his wrists, but even after resuming my original trail, I wasn't able to catch my original criminal. The damn man vanished into the night, melted into the dark, seedy underground, and didn't resurface again until he killed another innocent victim, which made murder number five." The horror and disappointment and guilt from that night came pouring back into his chest, filling it, tightening it, bringing self-loathing to taunt him once again.

"Oh, Hudson, I'm so sorry." She touched his arm, and that tiny bit of human connection had the power to push away the clinging darkness. "Was the case ever solved?"

"No." He shifted into a sitting position with one leg stretched out before him on the grass. "None of the other inspectors have been able to pin the killer down, and I didn't inquire. The next morning, I was reprimanded by my superiors for my inability to catch the murderer—regardless of the countless cases I had solved for Bow Street—and then I spent a few weeks recovering from my injuries. Perhaps I have the scars to serve as a reminder."

"Don't say that." Tears welled in her eyes. "You are a hero."

He snorted. "I certainly don't feel like one. While in my sickbed, I thought relentlessly about my career, about my failure and how differently the fellows at Bow Street regarded me, and eventually I resigned." A ball of emotion lodged in his throat. He cleared it and continued. "The poor woman who was the sister of the young lady slain was beside herself when I told her that I'd failed to apprehend the suspect. She cursed at me, railed, and eventually left my presence in a flurry of tears, which only firmed up my decision. I was past my prime."

"I don't believe that." Fierce passion threaded through her voice. Theodosia poked him in the chest with a gloved forefinger. "There were extenuating circumstances at play. Your superiors never gave you a chance."

Ah, her defense came dangerously close to making him a new man. He captured her hand. "Be that as it may, I doubt I will ever forgive myself for that failure. I had the chance to catch a criminal, but I didn't, so another victim fell." With a shrug, he looked away, suddenly not worthy of her regard. "Like a coward, I fled to Rome, wishing to be rid of my profession, the very thing I've an aptitude for."

"Yet fate intervened because the world still has use of you. Evil still lurks and it takes good men like you to stand up to it, to face it, and beat it back." She put a palm against the scarred side of his face and turned his head until their gazes met. "You didn't fail. *Life* failed *you*." Her chin quivered. "But you were here when *I* needed you, and I have every faith in you. So does Mrs. Claudian and my brother's housekeeper."

"Oh, God." To his horror, moisture sprang to his eyes. He hadn't shed a tear since that horrible night. "I don't deserve your praise or your regard, for I cannot guarantee success on your case... or any other." Never again could he bear to see the dawning horror and despair in another pair of eyes when a case went sideways.

"Stop it this instant." Silently, with her usual verve, she closed the distance, straddling his waist without regard to the state of her gown or the fact they could be imminently discovered at any moment. She put her face close to his. "I won't hear such talk."

"I don't want to disappoint anyone else." He forced down a hard swallow. "I don't want to be remembered as a pathetic man who lost his skill and his nerve." His voice broke, but he took refuge in her nearness and slipped his arms about her. "A man who hides."

"Then stop." Holding his head between her hands, she held his gaze, refused to look away. "Solve *this* case. Bring *my* child home. Regain *your* confidence. It's the only way to have the life you want so badly."

He edged a hand up her spine to rest at her nape. "I don't know if it's that simple."

"I didn't know if moving on, if continuing my life after I lost Nathaniel was simple either, and it wasn't," she admitted, and with each word, the warmth of her breath skated across his cheek. "Which is why it took me until now — last night in fact — to decide that I was ready to actually *live* again." Honesty shone in her eyes as she peered into his. "But it's the first step... and you deserve that, but only if you decide to stop being frightened and do it."

"Ah, Dia. How is it that I never knew of your presence in this city, not ten minutes walking distance from me, until now?" Then he dragged her to him and claimed her lips in a desperate, enlightened kiss that sent him tumbling impossibly, perhaps irrevocably, tip over tail for her after mere hours of meeting her.

Several minutes passed in heated wonder and innocent exploration, then the sound of raucous laughter and the clink of crystal drifted to his ears along with the word "tonight." With a huff of regret, he pulled away. When she would have protested, he pressed a finger to her lips. "Listen."

"Come to my masquerade tonight, my friend." That was Hanneford's voice, unexpectedly close. *Shit*, did they decide to walk in the garden? Panic welled his chest and he sat, frozen, with Theodosia still in his lap facing him. "It begins at ten o'clock, so you have just under four to prepare." Fabric rustled. Seconds later, the unmistakable sound of someone taking a piss very near to their location on the other side of the hedges met his ears.

He stared at Theodosia and shook his head, even as he wanted to gag in disgust. Especially when the man he'd brought with him did the same. She buried her face in the crook of his shoulder and shook with silent laughter.

"There will be enough women there to keep you busy for a fortnight. It will be my last social event while I'm in Rome, for I depart for England in a week." Finally, the streams of piss concluded, and fabric rustled again. "It is time to begin teaching my son what he'll need to be the marquess someday."

When Theodosia stiffened in his arms and opened her mouth to protest, Hudson quieted her with another kiss.

"I think I might, Hanneford." The clink of medals identified the second man as the host of the dinner party. "Especially since my wife has an engagement elsewhere tonight."

Ribald male laughter echoed and then faded slightly as they walked away, presumably to resume the remainder of their dinner.

This time, Theodosia broke the kiss. Anger and shock clouded her eyes, darkened in the fading sunlight. "This is our opportunity. I cannot lose *my* son to that man."

"And you won't." He arched an eyebrow. "Do you trust me?"

For long moments, she searched his face, and he hoped to God she found it. Then she nodded. "Yes. Implicitly."

A slow grin curved his mouth. "Then we have a masquerade ball to attend in four hours, and right now, we both look like rubbish." He winked. "I guess I'll be escorting you back home now."

The adventure was only just beginning.

Chapter Twelve

By the time Theodosia arrived back at Minerva Villa, she couldn't quite believe what had transpired in the last few hours, for it felt as if she'd already lived a lifetime.

"My lady!" Shock reverberated in Doris' voice as she came into the bedroom from the sitting room the same time Theodosia arrived from the corridor. "Whatever happened to you?" She immediately began fussing about the state of the gown, her hair, the smudges of dirt on her face, even wondered why the stockings and slippers were damp. "Are you well?" The other woman swiftly crossed the room and yanked on a velvet bell pull.

"Yes, of course, but I am in need of a bath as quickly as can be arranged." With a tiny sigh, she submitted into her maid's care as her gown was removed. "I am attending a masquerade ball tonight."

Doris stared. Her mouth opened and closed, but no words came out. Finally, she cleared her throat. "I beg your pardon? What about the investigator man? Has he found Jacob? I assumed that is what you were doing when you left earlier."

Heat seeped into Theodosia's cheeks. "Yes, among other things, but so much has happened since you and I spoke this morning that, as odd as it sounds, I am not the same woman I was then." She met her maid's gaze as she lowered her voice. "We need to talk candidly and privately."

Doris nodded. For the next few minutes, a porcelain tub was brought into the bedroom as Theodosia combed through both armoires in the adjoining room for a gown suitable for a masquerade ball. Dear heavens, she would need accessories. Could they even be procured at this late hour? Her thoughts went to Hudson. After he'd escorted her here, he'd gone on to his rooms with the promise of returning to the villa to take her to the ball.

And a vow that they wouldn't leave without having Jacob in hand.

Somehow, she believed him, for the former Bow Street man would never tell a lie and he wouldn't rest until his case was solved. The last one that had seen him retired and, in his mind, defeated had lit a fire under him for this one. She was certain of it.

And she admired that fierce determination, that unwavering belief he had of what was right and what was wrong... even if it put them at odds at times.

"My lady, your bath is ready," Doris said from the adjoining doorway.

"Thank you." Leaving a few gowns draped over various pieces of furniture, Theodosia entered the bedroom while tugging off the stays and then her stained and dirty petticoat. Finally, the stockings were abandoned. "This is much appreciated."

"What happened this afternoon?"

Once the clothes were removed, Theodosia slipped into the warm bath water and sighed. The faint scent of lilacs teased her nose. Immediately, Doris sat on a stool to one side of the tub, took up a porcelain pitcher, and proceeded to work on washing her hair.

Sparing the finer details of the afternoon, for she wished to keep those memories private and close to her heart, she related the happenings to the maid: receiving the threatening note with the emerald, being frightened and having Hudson go after her, walking through Roman neighborhoods, meeting his landlady, dinner at an outdoor café, spying on the marquess from a private garden, how they gained the knowledge that Hanneford was throwing a masquerade ball. The things they'd talked about that had nothing to do with

Jacob, she left out, and she certainly didn't relate that glorious hour she'd spent with him in his bed.

"Then you intend to bring the boy back home tonight." Surprise wove through Doris' voice. "Is it possible the marquess has your son in that villa where you will be?"

"Entirely possible and quite probable, actually." A thin ribbon of fear twisted up her spine. "We only have a handful of days to rescue him before the marquess takes him back to England." She forced down a hard swallow. "I don't know what he wants my son for, but I'd suspect his own child perished somehow. Perhaps he sent his wife away to have the babe; perhaps the death happened early in said child's life. I don't even know if his wife lives. Yet the man requires an heir as all titled men do, and he thinks taking Jacob is the easiest path."

"Dear God." Doris' hands shook as she washed Theodosia's hair. "He is devious."

"Indeed, he is. I shudder to think what will happen if Mr. Ridley and I don't succeed at this mission." She scrubbed at a streak of dirt on her arm with a soft sponge. "We must get Jacob back, even though Mr. Ridley tells me that you and I broke the law."

The maid scoffed. "Perhaps I did, but you kept me from basically leaving the child to die." She shook her head. "It's terrible what he ordered me to do and how desperately I needed to keep my position, so I did it." Her voice broke. "If it wasn't for you and Lord Ballantyne coming along when you did, I shudder to think of how that day might have gone."

"As do I." No, Jacob wasn't a child from her own loins, but that didn't mean she didn't love him as fiercely as if he were. "Hanneford never wanted the boy; never acknowledged him in any way. Someone in his household must have tattled that you didn't return from the errand he'd sent you on. How else would he have known Jacob still lived?"

"Men like him — powerful men — always have ways of knowing," Doris said with an ominous note to her voice. "He must be desperate to follow you all the way to Rome."

Knots of worry pulled in Theodosia's belly. "If that is true, and Mr. Ridley and I go after him, what will become of us if something goes wrong?" Hot panic welled in her chest. She clutched the edge of the tub as the urge to faint came over her. "Will he kill us and take Jacob anyway? Kill us so we don't talk?" As her breathing shallowed, she met her maid's gaze. "Will he send someone to come after you?"

They stared at each other as the possible horror dawned on them.

"Dear God." Doris quickly set the pitcher on the floor. "I never thought..."

"Me either. How stupid were we to assume we would never see him again?" As much as she wished Nathaniel was with her to take care of the potential problem, a wave of calm washed over her to know that Hudson would be by her side.

Eventually, Theodosia rose from the bath water and Doris wrapped her in a towel. "I cannot think of failures right now. We have to assume Hudson, er, Mr. Ridley and I will be successful in getting Jacob back."

"What if Hanneford comes after you?"

She shrugged. "I cannot fathom."

A knowing light appeared in the maid's eyes. "What happened between you and the Bow Street man you aren't telling me? Remember, my lady, I have known you for eight years."

Another round of heat went through Theodosia's cheeks. "He is the man I hired to find my son. A lovely man, at that." It was all she would admit to.

The maid snorted. "There is nothing wrong in finding yourself attracted to another man. Lord Ballantyne has been gone for three years."

For one moment, Theodosia wished to confess all to the maid, but she couldn't. It was all still so new and confusing, and at the heart of the matter was the knowledge that she had only known Hudson for a day. What did it say of her character of what she'd already done with the man? "Thank you for the reminder, Doris."

"If he makes you happy, though, my lady—"

"Hush."

"He's not overtly handsome with that scar but he is probably fiercely loyal."

Theodosia frowned, for she found Hudson attractive in body and soul. "Oh, Doris, please let us drop the subject." Frissons of need danced down her spine as she thought of him. The truth was, she simply wasn't ready to analyze anything relating to Hudson just yet. There was still too much uncertainty surrounding her son. Rescuing him was her first priority. She headed into the adjoining dressing room. "It is too early to figure out what he is to me, or what I want him to be."

"Not if what it is already between you feels right," Doris said as she followed. "There is something different about you that wasn't there this morning." When Theodosia didn't answer, the maid chuckled. "Isn't it better to simply close your eyes and leap? Besides, he would be a good man for Jacob to see as he grows into adolescence."

That was quite true, but if something untoward happened that prevented Jacob's safe return... "We shall revisit that later. For now, let us turn our attention to what I should wear to the masquerade. No sense in having Hanneford recognize me straightaway, hmm?"

It took a bit of contriving and imagination, but between her and Doris, they concocted a costume worthy of any masquerade ball and one that didn't look like it had been thrown together.

"Good heavens, this is amazing." Theodosia peered at herself in the full-length cheval glass, turning this way and that while admiring the affect. "I cannot believe you were able to do this."

The gown of gold satin was cool where it touched her skin. An overskirt of delicate white lace decorated with hundreds of tiny clear glass beads. It sparkled with her every movement. The same lace lined the low bodice and the edges of the short, capped sleeves. Around her throat was a gold circlet of plain, solid metal perhaps an inch wide. It was one of the last gifts Nathaniel had given her before he died, calling her his angel as he'd done so.

But what made the costume so amazing were the large gossamer-like wings hastily constructed of the sheerest white silk and outlined with feathers plucked from a few pillows. It was a wonder both she and Doris didn't have glue and feathers stuck to their persons. A plain golden tiara completed her ensemble, and though it wasn't a halo, one could pretend.

They'd even managed to root up a white domino mask and glued a few feathers to that as well.

For the time being, the wonderous wings lay draped over a winged-back chair, waiting for the time they would need strapping onto her shoulders.

Truly, she had transformed herself into an angel, as an unconscious tribute to her dead husband. *Oh, you would have adored the adventure, I think.*

"I would say we've outdone ourselves." Doris clasped her hands in front of her and grinned like a fool. "If you were attending the ball with the intention of snaring a gentleman's interest, this gown would certainly accomplish that."

Theodosia's own grin faltered. "I am not, so it might shield me from the marquess' notice for long enough to accomplish my task." What would Hudson think of the costume? Would he find her fascinating, enchanting?

Did she want him to?

"No doubt it will."

A knock on the sitting room door preceded the arrival of Theodosia's brother.

Doris caught her eye. "Ring if you need me. I'll just go root through the trunk in your bedchamber for the pair of golden slippers."

"Thank you." Then she turned her attention to Thomas. "I'm surprised to see you. Don't you have an engagement this evening?"

"I do, rather, but when I was apprised that you had returned, I wish to have a word." He glanced at her and then nodded. "You are certainly well turned out tonight."

She offered a tight smile. "I am attending the Marquess of Hanneford's masquerade ball. It is to be his last social event, for he leaves for England soon." None of that was a lie and it was easily acquired, so she didn't mind informing him of such.

"Ah." He clasped his hands behind his back. "I wasn't aware you knew Hanneford."

Yes, the bloody man might be higher on the instep than she or her brother, but then that wasn't the reason she was acquainted with him. Not even her brother knew of Jacob's true lineage. And now wasn't the time to tell him, for he would forbid her to go. "In passing only." Another truth.

Thomas frowned. "What happened to you?"

That was a rather broad question. "Whatever do you mean?" It seemed as if the events of the day had occurred ages ago.

"I mean that Jacob is still missing, but you were out of the villa much of the afternoon."

"What of it? I was investigating."

"With that Bow Street fellow. That Mr. Ridley." It wasn't a question.

"Yes, of course. Who else?" Not allowing her brother the chance to answer, she plunged onward. "We walked the streets close to the villa, questioned the mother of the boy who'd said he'd been taken. Then we looked about the area for more clues." She shrugged and returned her attention to the cheval glass. "It was all very interesting."

Another truth though some of those things had surpassed expectations.

"Yet Jacob hasn't been found." One of his eyebrows rose in question.

"While this is correct, Mr. Ridley and I are going after him tonight."

Thomas snorted. "At a masquerade ball?"

"Yes, of course." She cut the air with a hand. "It is a long, convoluted explanation that is best kept until after his safe return."

"Poppycock." His frown deepened. "There is something else." He narrowed his eyes. "Something you are not telling me."

"I rather think there isn't." Theodosia turned away from the looking glass lest he see the heat that blazed in her cheeks. "Searching for clues has kept me quite busy this afternoon." To say nothing of being in Hudson's company, learning about him, discovering what had shaped him into the man that he was. Besides, she couldn't very well blurt out to her brother that she'd been thoroughly bedded by the former Bow Street man, and what was more, she'd enjoyed herself immensely.

Goodness, but he would lock her in her rooms, give her a lecture regarding proper deportment while on the Continent, and then tell her she would be meeting a few of his friends who were in need of a wife.

To knock the silly notions from her head and keep her out of trouble, no doubt.

"No, I stand by my original statement." He took a few steps forward, put a hand on her shoulders, and turned Theodosia about to face him. "There is something… different about you tonight."

"I cannot imagine what."

"You seem happy."

She frowned. "There is nothing wrong with that."

"Of course not, but you should be shattered with Jacob missing. Quite frankly, I don't know how you are holding yourself together." Though compassion threaded through his voice, confusion clouded his eyes. "What the devil happened to you this afternoon that has changed apparently everything?"

"I am quite upset my son is still missing, but I'm seeking to rectify that. With the clues Mr. Ridley and I found today, we are close to a resolution." A bit of hysterical laughter escaped her. There was still that undercurrent of attraction, of desire, that connected her and Hudson each time they were together. "Quite frankly, brother dear, you wouldn't believe me if I tried to explain to you what has happened to me today."

Thomas stepped away and once more peered at her, looking her up and down as if he couldn't quite figure her out. "The butler told me you looked like a fallen woman at a war refugee camp when you came in an hour ago."

"Yes, well, the butler should mind his own business." She couldn't keep the frostiness from her tone, and not wishing to be that close to her brother lest he guess the truth, she moved across the room to the window. "The streets of Rome teem with dirt and filth of all kinds. You know that. It is only natural my hem was dirtied. As for the stains on the skirt... I fell into one of my faints when allowing the panic of not being able to find Jacob to get the better of me."

Not quite a lie. Even Thomas knew of her affliction for blackouts.

"I am sorry to hear that. Do your lungs still pain you?"

"Not since I have been in Rome. I suspect London is too dirty and polluted for me to breathe comfortably; I am not looking forward to returning." But eventually, she must because of Jacob's future.

"Yes, well, there is that. I am glad you are none the worse for wear though." Doubt threaded through his words. "It is good that Mr. Ridley accompanied you on those outings."

"Indeed." And it was that penchant for fainting which had led them to other, more interesting activities beyond mere comfort. "However, for the moment I am quite well if a bit apprehensive." She smoothed her hands over her skirting. "Everything hinges on tonight, Thomas." Then she turned, sought out his gaze and hoped he would understand everything she couldn't tell him. "Please know we will do all that we can to have Jacob back."

"Of course you will. I didn't mean to hint that you won't."

Before she could answer or he could add to his statement, a knock rang on the door. They both glanced up. The butler stood in the frame.

"What is it, Carruthers?" Thomas asked with a trace of irritation in his expression.

"There is a Mr. Ridley in the drawing room, Ambassador."

"Oh!" Another round of heat went through Theodosia's cheeks. "I should finish donning my costume then."

The butler cleared his throat and shook his head. "Mr. Ridley has asked to speak with your brother, my lady. He says there is some business which needs discussing before he escorts you to the ball."

"Ah." She exchanged a baffled glance with Thomas. "Do you know that is about?"

"I do not, but how interesting." He beheld the butler. "I shall be down directly. Thank you." Once Carruthers departed, her brother sighed. "Be careful tonight. One member of my family is missing. I'd rather not have another meet the same fate. However would I explain it to Percy?"

Theodosia pointed her gaze to the ceiling. "You are the diplomat. I'm sure you could manage." She made a shooing motion with her hand. "Go. I have a toilette to finish." Yet butterflies danced a ballet in her lower belly, for she couldn't wait to see Hudson again. They would find Jacob tonight, she could just feel it.

Chapter Thirteen

It wasn't often that Hudson was beset with nerves, but the longer he waited in the ambassador's drawing room, the more his skin seemed to crawl with them.

After he'd returned to his lodgings from escorting Theodosia home, he'd torn apart his clothespress and drawers to piece together some sort of costume for tonight's ball. The only thing he could remotely come up with was a vague highwayman. And even that was a stretch. Outside of appearing at the marquess' residence in a bedsheet draped about his body as a makeshift toga, that was as good as it would get.

With nothing for it, he'd had a quick bath in a wooden tub much too short and shallow for his bulk, explained the whole of the situation to Mrs. Claudian—who insisted on helping him bathe for Christ's sake and then acted as his valet after that—he'd taken himself off to the ambassador's residence in order to collect Theodosia.

Now, as he quietly paced the floor in front of two sets of windows thrown open to catch the night breeze, he contemplated what the devil he was even doing asking for an audience with her brother. But he couldn't put this meeting off any longer. Yes, he'd known Theodosia for a day only, but he had distinct feelings for her that went beyond lust and desire. He admired her bravery and courage, her determination and compassion, her unwavering pursuit of what she thought was right.

When they'd lain in the gardens and spied on Hanneford, he'd wished to tell her how he was feeling, but he'd been too much a coward, especially after telling her about his last case and being a touch vulnerable. But now, just being parted with her for a meager two hours in order to prepare for the ball, he knew one thing above all certainty. He wished to pay his addresses to her if she would have him, if she didn't mind the societal divide between them. Yet the decision was impossible and irrational, but surprising and affirming.

In Theodosia's company, he felt alive again after two years of feeling quite dead inside. Now, he had a purpose again, a reason to venture out of his rooms, something to look forward to beyond a bottle of brandy and talking to his cat.

Damn, so much had changed in a twenty-four period. Did the meeting of one woman have that much power?

Obviously, it did. He was living proof, but he wanted everything legitimate and out in the open, and that meant doing the pretty with her brother, asking for his permission in lieu of being able to talk with her older brother, Percy, or even her father, wherever he may be.

"Ah, Mr. Ridley."

Hudson whirled about at the sound of the ambassador's voice. "Ambassador Netherton. I am glad you have agreed to this meeting." It was obvious the man was Theodosia's sibling; they had similar looks, but Dia had softer edges and a brighter smile.

"I can see you are anxious to be off, dressed as you are." The other man swept his gaze up and down Hudson's form, taking in the black breeches and boots, the linen shirt with the loose sleeves, the crimson length of satin about his waist borrowed from Mrs. Claudian to make—in her words—the "costume look authentic" as well as the black domino mask clutched tightly in his hand.

"Time *is* rather of the essence."

"Come." The ambassador gestured him over to a grouping of furniture, and when Thomas sat in a chair, Hudson dropped into one across a low table from him. "What can I do for you, Mr. Ridley? Have you an update on the case of my missing nephew?"

"Yes and no." He went to tug at his cravat knot, but then he remembered he wasn't wearing that particular piece of clothing tonight. "We have determined who took the boy and will retrieve the child tonight." He didn't know if she had told her brother the truth about Jacob's lineage, but he would keep her secret.

One of Thomas' eyebrows rose in challenge. "We?"

"Yes." He cleared his throat. "Theodosia and I. Er, Lady Ballantyne." Heat rose on the back of his neck as the other man stared. "It has been a busy, full day, so we dispensed with the formalities."

"I see. Simple enough, then. I wish you luck." The ambassador rested an ankle on a knee and then clasped his hands before him. "That isn't why you wanted this audience, is it?"

"Not quite." Hudson fidgeted, shifted his weight in the chair. He shoved the fingers of one hand through his hair. Oh, Mrs. Claudian would be displeased to see how he destroyed the work she'd put into setting it. "It seems I have developed certain… feelings for your sister." A hard swallow did not alleviate a suddenly dry throat. "Romantic feelings, I should clarify."

"Ah. So then you believe you are in love with Theodosia." It wasn't a question, but there was a hard set to Thomas' chin and a rather narrowing of his eyes Hudson didn't quite trust.

"If you wish for me to put a descriptor on it, yes, I suppose that's correct." Now that he'd said it aloud, it sounded even more outrageous. He was a man of logic, damn it. If he couldn't see it with his own eyes, he rarely believed it. Yet, there was no explaining that connection. They'd met the night before. It had been a day, but in some ways, it felt as if he'd already lived a lifetime with her and that hadn't been enough. He wanted so much more.

"Well, Mr. Ridley, let me ask you a few questions so we can better narrow down those elusive feelings of you, hmm?" The ambassador unbent to plant both feet on the floor, rest his forearms on his knees, and let his hands dangle between his legs. "Perhaps I am overprotective of my sister, but she is in a vulnerable state right now."

Hudson snorted. "She is much stronger than you suspect." With every hour that went by, with each new revelation, he remained in awe of her.

"Be that as it may, I find it difficult to think of anyone being in love after a day." The doubt reflected in the ambassador's eyes. "Ask yourself these questions before you protest, Mr. Ridley." The other man held up a forefinger. Apparently, he would tick them all off. "When disagreeing with Theodosia, if those harsh words you say to her and make her eyes wells with tears don't make *your* throat burn as if you just downed a bottle of whiskey, you are *not* in love with her."

"We *have* argued..." And though the other man had a valid point, he'd hated to see those emotions march across her face.

Again, the ambassador cocked an eyebrow. "If her eyes cannot make you falter in your steps or steal the breath from your lungs, you are *not* in love with her." He held up three fingers. "If your words trip over themselves while trying to talk to her, if the scent of her perfume doesn't make you daydream, you are *not* in love with her."

Hudson crossed his arms at his chest. "I really don't see how any of this is your business."

Thomas continued as if he wasn't interrupted. "If Theodosia's laugh doesn't make you clench your hands until your knuckles turn white or tense your chest at the thought of never hearing it again because you've been an arse, you are *not* in love with her." He narrowed his eyes on Hudson and held up another finger. "If my sister's voice cannot calm your worst anxiety or you don't keep her talking merely to hear that voice, you *aren't* in love with her."

"You have a point, Ambassador." He *did* adore listening to Theodosia talk. "She is quite... something."

The man allowed a faint grin. "If her smile doesn't make you wish to expire but feel as if you were born again in the same breath, you are *not* in love with her." He dusted an invisible piece of lint from his suit coat. "And finally, if you only wish to remove her from her clothing or dallying with her in bed is when you pay the most attention to her — not that this last point applies to your situation considering the short amount of time you've known her — you are *not* in love with her."

Heat built in Hudson's chest. How dare this man try to assume what there was between him and Theodosia! It didn't matter that they'd already shared the greatest intimacy. There was an indefinable connection between them. None of that had bearing on this present conversation. If the ambassador knew about that, he'd run Hudson off without another word.

Slowly, he rose to his feet, and Hudson had no choice but to scramble to his. "So, Mr. Ridley, you can see how doubtful I am that your words ring true."

"Frankly, Ambassador, this meeting was merely a formality." Anger slashed through his chest. "I would like to pay my addresses to your sister, and we are both past an age where we might need your permission, but my intentions *are* pure toward her."

Something flickered over the ambassador's face that he couldn't identify. For long moments, silence reigned between them then Thomas shook his head. "No."

"No? As I said, I don't need your permission, but your support would have been a lovely extension of trust and faith."

"Just what I said, Mr. Ridley. No." His face was impassive as he crossed his arms at his chest. "Regardless of how you answer the questions I've already asked of you, I rather think you aren't good enough for Theodosia."

Those were the words he'd feared hearing since that last damned case, and each one felt like a blow to the breadbasket. "I..." What else could he say?

"Beyond that, you are decidedly not of her social class. Without an income, how can you keep her in the style in which she has become accustomed?" The ambassador edged to the door. "My sister is a viscountess; she is the mother of a future viscount. Her place will always be in London society, and you are hardly a piece that fits into that picture."

"There is more to life—more to love— than being compatible in society or how much coin one has in the bank or how sterling their connections." In fact, love didn't care about any of that. It simply... was. "As to the income bit, once this case has concluded, I plan to offer my services as a retrieval expert privately. To help where the authorities don't want to or can't. There seems to be quite a need." He shrugged but narrowed his eyes on the ambassador. "What I charge for such services, is none of your concern. As it is I have paid up my lease on my rooms through the end of the year, as per usual, so it's not as if I'm a layabout."

"Yet you left Bow Street in disgrace, did you not?"

Another blow. Pain went through his chest, and he stumbled backward a couple of steps. How had the man known that? Perhaps his connections ran deep. Then annoyance stabbed into him, hot and accurate. "That has no bearing here, and it's in my past besides." When he realized he was clenching one of his hands into a fist, he forced himself to relax. "However, since being in Rome, I have been the epitome of responsibility. I'm certain my landlady can vouch for me."

I must truly be desperate if I've added that.

The ambassador snorted. "You drink."

Hudson glared. "Who among us doesn't?"

Not to be outdone, the other man continued. "You have had women in your bed, I'll wager."

Including your sister. He tamped the urge to laugh in the other man's face. "What sort of interrogation is this, then?" It bordered on too personal. If the ambassador insisted on being snide, then the sentiment would be returned. "I never claimed I was a monk, and neither are you, hmm?"

There was frost in the ambassador's eyes, that were much the same color as Theodosia's. "Eventually, my sister will return to England for her son's future. If you follow her, you will need to start your life over without support. It will be difficult considering old stories and rumors will resurface to threaten that livelihood."

"And no doubt unearthed by you? All in a bid to protect her?" he asked in a quiet voice, but damn, he hadn't thought of that.

The ambassador's shrug only lifted on shoulder. "Does it matter?"

"No, I suppose it doesn't." He narrowed his eyes. "I love your sister, Ambassador. That means something." The strength in his voice behind those words made him proud, and this time it was the ambassador who took a step away.

"Such an emotion is meaningless without a plan or a future for yourself. If you were to marry, my sister and her son cannot live in rented rooms. They deserve more."

"Agreed, but—"

"It is in your best interest—and hers—to cut ties once this case is solved," the other man continued as if Hudson hadn't spoken. He continued his movement across the room until he stood at the doorway and stared pointedly at him. "This will prevent you from breaking her heart, for I will *not* stand for that."

"As if I would ever do anything to hurt her."

One of the ambassador's eyebrows lifted again. "Is there anything else, Mr. Ridley? I'm afraid I have an engagement yet tonight."

The man was a prick, this was true, but Hudson couldn't blame him for wishing to see Theodosia protected. It was something they both had in common. "No." Stunned and with cold defeat swirling through his gut, he had no choice but to exit the room. In the corridor, he said, "Thank you for the time. I'm sure you will have your nephew back shortly after midnight." When the other man said nothing, Hudson heaved out a frustrated breath. "In the event you wondered, I would die to protect your sister. How many of the men you wish for her to meet would do that?"

Uncertainty crossed the ambassador's face, and Hudson resisted the urge to crow with that small victory. As he made his way down the grand staircase to the foyer below, the breath whooshed from his lungs to see Theodosia standing there, clearly waiting for him.

She is so beautiful!

Just like the angel she pretended to be tonight. He gawked at the gold and white confection she'd donned, was astounded at the gossamer feathery wings attached to her back by loops over her shoulders. Took in the golden tiara atop her blonde hair that had been piled on her head and secured with pins that sparkled with tiny chips of diamonds. Each time she moved, something on her outfit sparkled and shone until he was convinced he was, indeed, in the presence of a member of the heavenly host.

"Dear God, you are an angel." He rested a hand over his heart. "Have I died, then?"

"It is what my husband used to call me."

"He had the right of it, then." The tinkling giggle she loosed into the air went straight to his stones. It was adorable how she acted with each tiny compliment. Theodosia flashed a wide smile. "You guessed what my costume is. My maid will be pleased." She held up a gloved hand where a matching domino mask dangled. "Do you think Hanneford will be fooled?"

"For a time." Hudson shrugged. This woman was a delight; she brought light to his existence. "Truly, you are beautiful. I can't stop staring." The satiny skin of her slender neck fairly called out to him. What he wouldn't do to kiss the crook of her shoulder, nibble a path beneath her ear.

How could he call an end to their association once her son was safely back home? The ambassador could hate him all he wanted, but Hudson would only leave her side if Theodosia herself asked him to.

"You already said that to me earlier today when I wasn't wearing this costume," she said in a low voice that sent heat skittering down his spine. "Now I wonder which one is really true."

Dear God.

"Uh…" What the devil should he say to that? "Every word I've said to you today has been true. It matters not what you wear or how you look. I will always think you are beautiful."

"Who knew an ex-Bow Street man knew how to flirt?" She touched the edge of her mask to his chest as she raked her gaze up and down his person. "I rather like this devil-may-care look on you." She came near, lifted onto her toes, fit her lips to his ear and whispered, "I have always had a weakness for highwaymen. Can you imagine what that must have been like when they bedeviled English roads and lanes?"

Would that they were alone. "It is too bad I can't whisk you into a shadowy corner and demand your valuables or your virtue."

"Mmm." Her eyes darkened slightly, but then she frowned. "What is wrong?"

"What do you mean?"

"You seem troubled. I can see it in your face." Theodosia laid her free hand on his chest. "What has occurred?"

"Nothing." His lungs seized, for he couldn't tell her what her brother had said. It would only cause trouble between the siblings. When his heart squeezed as he thought about not seeing her past the conclusion of the case, he gasped in pain. "I'm fine so don't worry. Perhaps I'm merely on edge for what we still need to do tonight." No, she didn't need to know of his feelings, for in doing so it would only hurt her.

Unless she didn't return that sentiment, and how could she? It had been a day. He would walk away gracefully once the case was done—for the sake of her future.

"Oh." Yet she wasn't convinced, for she was too intelligent. "You seem sad, Hudson. Is it because of me? Of this case?"

"No." *Damn it all.* He refused to destroy their remaining time together even if they were on a mission. "Please don't worry about it. We have a ball to crash." Hopefully, he'd infused enough lightheartedness into his voice she'd be convinced. "And if I'm fortunate, perhaps you will dance with me." Holding her in his arms on the dance floor would have to be enough to last a real lifetime. No matter that he wanted to rail at the heavens—at her brother—facts were facts.

"I would enjoy that very much."

"Good." He had his world and she belonged in hers. If he was only allotted his one night, he wouldn't waste it. Offering her his bent arm, he nearly died a thousand deaths as she rested her gloved hand atop his sleeve. "Let us pray we are successful. I want you to welcome in the dawn with Jacob at your side."

It was the least he could do to make her happy before he had to give her up.

Chapter Fourteen

Theodosia commandeered her brother's open carriage for their conveyance tonight. When he'd objected, she'd waved him off and said she would send it back so he could take it to his engagement. For whatever reason, when Hudson exchanged a look with Thomas, her brother had abandoned the argument with a shrug.

It was another odd occurrence in a night of such strangeness, for something was bothering Hudson even though he'd assured her he was fine. Even now, as they exited the vehicle, he was moody and quiet, had hardly spoken ten words to her on the ride to Hanneford's villa. In fact, it was almost as if the man had fallen into despair in the short time they'd been parted to prepare for the ball.

Then she sucked in a breath as she tied the strings of her masquerade mask behind her head. "What was your meeting with my brother about?"

Hudson flinched as if she'd struck him. Since they'd left the carriage a bit down the street from the villa, they needed to walk. When she assumed he would ignore the question, he merely took her gloved hand and threaded it through his crooked elbow. "This and that. Mostly he wanted to know about progress on the case."

"Was he pleased to know that Jacob will be home sometime tonight?"

A sound suspiciously like a grunt escaped him. "He didn't comment."

Of course he didn't. Theodosia frowned. "What else did he say?"

A muscle in Hudson's cheek ticced while he donned his own domino mask. "He's concerned about your future."

"Pish posh. I can make my own decisions." Though she took exception to Thomas' highhandedness, she was more concerned about Hudson. "Did you and he argue?"

"I can honestly say we did not." A ghost of a grin graced his lips as they strolled in the balmy night toward the villa where golden light illuminated every window. "There were a few times I had a different opinion than he, but in the end, there was nothing I could do about it."

That made absolutely no sense, but since it didn't appear the former investigator wished to talk, she sighed. Why were men so difficult to understand? Even after being married to one, she still didn't know what their many moods meant. "You are quite dashing this evening. If society would relax its rigid laws and more men went about dressed in shirtsleeves, it might be a more pleasant world."

A tiny snort of laughter escaped him. "Certainly, a more interesting one, but I don't see any society relaxing those rules in our lifetime." When he chuckled, the sound tickled through her chest. "Imagine men and women running about outside their homes in some state of undress that bares their legs and shows parts of their chests. There would be chaos."

For a moment, the thought of Hudson's naked legs and chest being on display took over every section of her brain. "If the people involved were attractive enough, nothing would ever be accomplished. I agree."

A hoot of his laughter echoed on the air. "Now imagine a man shaped like the Regent in such attire. How would you feel then?"

A picture of the corpulent, rotund Prinny jumped into her mind. A shiver of revulsion shot down her spine. "No thank you. Perhaps I'm glad of society's rules after all."

"Ah, Dia, you are adorable. Did you know that?" Briefly, he pulled her close into his side but then released her as they approached the front walkway that led to the villa's door. "You will make some lucky man a wonderful wife."

Warmth went through her cheeks from both his words and his touch. Then she frowned. "Is that what Thomas told you? That he's selected a handful of men for me to meet? To pick for someone to wed?" A pox on her brother! She needed none of his friends or acquaintances. If she were honest with herself, the only person she wanted was Hudson.

Then the enormity of what this night meant slammed into her chest. Once Jacob was home safe, what would become of the former Bow Street man? Would she ever see him again? The knowledge that she might not had sadness welling through her chest, ready to swallow her whole.

"Theodosia? Is all well? Are you feeling faint?"

Of course he was ever aware of her changing moods. It was one of the things she appreciated about him. She squeezed her fingers on his arm. "It's nothing."

"You are not a very good liar," he whispered into her ear as they gained entry into the house among a large knot of other people.

"Neither are you." Theodosia refused to look at him, couldn't really through the slits of her mask.

"I am trained to be such."

"Not to the people who know you best," she said over her shoulder at him. His hand at the small of her back as he guided her through the crush was distracting. "Something bothers you, but you refuse to share."

"It's not something I wish to burden you with. Please drop the subject." A note of warning lingered in his voice. Then they were through the knot of costumed guests who laughed and chattered, none of them concerned with life or its complications. Since they'd arrived a half hour late, there was no receiving line, thank goodness, so they wouldn't come face to face with the marquess just yet. "Now, let us get our bearings and make a plan."

"Right." Theodosia nodded. It was good to have something solid to focus on, but she couldn't help but feel he was shutting her out little by little.

Why?

Not knowing and with a hard knot of worry in her belly, she followed him over to the side of the entry hall. "Where do you think the marquess is holding Jacob?"

Hudson briefly perked up. A light of interest appeared in his eyes. "No doubt in an upstairs room or suite. There will probably be a guard, so we'll need to be on ours."

She appreciated the play on words but couldn't bring herself to smile. "Even if

Hanneford doesn't know that *we* know the boy is here?"

"Guilty men always have precautions." He scanned his gaze over the party guests that passed their location. "We'll need to be extremely cautious."

"Of course." Theodosia's pulse quickened. They were so close to the goal. "Will the rescue and escape prove too difficult?" Surely, they wouldn't be denied.

"I hope not." Hudson shrugged and focused his attention back on her. "However, neither of us are alone on this mission, so there's that." A ghost of a grin but there were haunted shadows in his eyes. "We should move toward the ballroom."

"All right." What was he thinking about that had him so distracted and would it affect his performance with the rescue? "For what it's worth, I am glad you are here with me." She caught his hand, squeezed his gloved fingers. "In fact, I am thrilled I met you." Perhaps it wasn't a good time for the admittance, but she didn't want to lose her chance. This day had been one of the most amazing of her life, had made her feel alive again and wanted despite the reason for their meeting.

This time his grin was the one she'd come to expect. "So am I." He held onto her hand regardless of the crush of guests in the corridor. "Being able to dance with you before the case ends will be the pinnacle of success, since you enjoy the exercise so much."

"That's sweet." Heat burned through her cheeks. "Thank you for remembering."

"Always with anything about you." He guided her past the grand staircase of marble toward the ballroom. "Shall we begin the mission?"

Twin trembles of unease and anticipation twisted up her spine. "I suppose that would be best. No sense in letting it drag out." Except, concluding the case left her with more questions than answers, the greatest of which was what would become of their relationship.

By the time they filtered into the ballroom with a knot of other costumed guests, polite applause from the people already inside met her ears. It seemed they'd missed Hanneford's welcome speech as well as the opening country reel. She sucked in a breath the moment her gaze landed on the man, who had come dressed as a pirate of old, complete with a floppy hat that had an ostrich feather stuck in the brim. Knee boots were folded over and there was a pistol slung low over his hips. Was that a real weapon or merely a prop?

Hudson squeezed her fingers. "I see him, but for the moment, he doesn't see us. Which gives us the advantage." Even still, he pulled the brim of his hat a bit lower down to hide the scars on his cheek.

"What should we do now?" She wanted to rush at the man, demand he tell her where he'd hidden her son, but alternately wished to hide away from the fight she felt was coming. None of this was what she'd wanted for her life, but then if it hadn't happened, she would never have met the former Bow Street man.

And that was rather unbearable.

"When one is conflicted, the best way to clear the mind is to focus on doing something else entirely. Let us join this set." Then he led her out onto the floor, found an open spot, and whisked her into his arms.

"Oh!" A thrill came over her as she assumed the proper form for what would be a Vienna style waltz. She'd missed that, the feeling of safety and security that being in his embrace offered. Doing so now reminded her of how she'd felt in his arms earlier when they'd talked in the gardens, when they'd nearly given way to passion yet again, how close they'd drawn together merely by sharing their truths.

That was how any romantic relationship should begin and feel like, wasn't it?

Then the string quartet's opening notes floated upon the air and Hudson started them into motion with the first steps of the dance.

Due to the complicated nature of the set, she was only partnered with him part of the time, but whenever she came back with him, he wasn't inclined to talk. Honestly, there were no need for words when his eyes said everything his lips didn't. Never had she passed such a magical time on a dance floor.

Every time their hands brushed, lightning edged down her spine. The looks they exchanged when coming back together could set fire to the room. She swore his every movement was exaggerated so that various parts of his body touched hers at some point to further fan those flames. Whenever her gaze met his and held, pieces of her soul flew into his keeping, and she received the same from him. Did he feel that strong connection? That feeling of belonging? Such was what she'd experienced when she'd met Nathaniel, and they had been wonderfully happy until his violent death. Could it be so with Hudson? When next she came together with him and their hands touched, their gazes met again, silent promises were hinted at in his ice blue eyes that sent need shuddering through her lower belly.

Oh, what she wouldn't do to have him alone! To talk and kiss and plan with. This man had completely upended her life in one day and she suddenly didn't want that to end.

But everything had an end point, and this waltz was no different. As it wound to a conclusion and polite applause filled the air, Hudson put a hand to the small of her back and his lips to her ear.

"We are going upstairs now in the confusion of switching sets. Use the back stairs and once on the upper levels, we'll do quick surveillance." Despite the thrilling rumble of his voice, she concentrated on his words and nodded. "Soon you will have Jacob in your arms, my lady."

The thought brought tears to her eyes, but there was no time to give into them. As unobtrusively as she could, she followed Hudson from the room, and attempted to act naturally as she walked along the corridor toward the rear of the house. Once they gained the staircase primarily used by the servants, she breathed a quick sigh of relief and tailed him up to the first landing.

"What about you, Hudson?" she couldn't help but ask in a whisper, made him pause with a hand on his arm in the shadows. Eventually, her son would need schooling and lessons on how to be a man in the *ton*, but was she hoping for a future with the retired Bow Street man? Didn't those desires war with each other? "What are your plans after this?" They had only met a day ago, but the thought of never seeing him again brought out a wave panic that filled her chest.

One long day fraught with a gambit of emotions. A day that seemed a lifetime already. A day that had shaken her very existence and rattled the foundations of her life.

How could she forget any of it with a return to daily schedules?

He turned to her, swallowing heavily. The shadows in his eyes frightened her, but the determined set to his mouth gave her a modicum of hope. "I promise we will think of something," he assured in in a barely audible whisper. "Right now, we have to move lest we're found out."

Theodosia nodded, but the worry didn't leave her stomach.

Once they gained the third level where the bedrooms were located, she was surprised to note there weren't guards stationed in front of the doors. Was that good or bad? Three doors reposed on each side of the corridor.

She glanced at Hudson, who shrugged. They went door by door in silence but were met with empty rooms devoid of occupancy for the moment. At the last door, Hudson tugged her aside, took her into his arms, and gave her such a gentle kiss that it brought another round of tears to her eyes.

"I wanted to say it has been an honor working for you—with you—today. I never expected to share as much as I did with you or do anything else either." A dark flush crept over the loose yoke of his shirt as he peered down into her face. "All of it is something I'll never forget." Emotion graveled his voice, and she felt it rise in her throat as well.

She curled a hand into the fabric of his shirt. A sense of loss came over her as she frowned. "This *isn't* goodbye, Hudson." But it certainly wasn't the time to tell him how she was beginning to feel, what he meant to her. Not while her attention was split between him and having her son back with her.

Slowly, he nodded and released her. "In the event that things go south, I will create a diversion so you can escape with your boy," he said in a barely there whisper.

Her heart trembled. "No. We go together or not at all."

Amusement danced briefly in his eyes, gone when he shook his head. "It is what is required of me."

Oh, he would be stubborn to the last. "Do you have a pistol?"

"No, but there's a knife in my boot and I'll find a weapon if needed."

This couldn't—wouldn't—be the end of them together. She wouldn't let it. Not knowing what to say, she closed the slight distance between them, pushed onto her toes, and then pressed her lips to his. "For luck," she managed in a broken whisper.

"To you as well." He cocked an eyebrow. "Let's go."

Theodosia nodded. She pressed the doorlatch and pushed open the panel. The sound of a tin bell echoed in the silence of the corridor, and then all chaos broke loose.

"Mama!" Jacob flew off a chair and over the floor to fling himself into her arms.

At the same time, a burly man obviously planted to make certain the boy didn't escape took one look at Hudson and immediately engaged him in a fist fight.

The first blow clipped the Bow Street man on the shoulder, but he retaliated by firing off an uppercut to the other man's chin. He spared her a glance. "Run! Take the boy and disappear into the streets of Rome!" That tiny distraction earned him a punch to the jaw that had him reeling backward and fighting for his footing.

"Hudson!" She clung to Jacob's shaking form and was determined not to leave Hudson to his fate, but when another man entered the sitting room from an adjoining bedroom, fate made the decision for her. As the sounds of scuffling filled her ears, she took Jacob's hand. "Quickly, out the window."

"But Mama…"

"No complaining. That man over there is risking his life for you — for us. Don't make it be in vain." There was no time to think about the consequences of such a rash action or if Hudson would indeed make it out of the room alive.

After dashing across the room and throwing the window panels wide open, Theodosia climbed out first. One of her angel wings got snagged, but she ripped it off and then planted her slippered feet on a stone ledge about three feet below the window. "Jacob, come." She couldn't think of the danger she or her son faced. If she did, panic would take over, and if she fainted, she would topple off the side of the building.

When the boy climbed out the window as lithe as a monkey and joined her on the ledge, she spared a glance back into the room. Hudson fought against the two men, and they'd backed him literally into a corner. Glass shattered, and the sound of something heavy hitting the floor met her ears as she turned away and concentrated on the task at hand — moving along the way-too-narrow ledge into order to access a piece of flat roof that would eventually lead to a vine-covered trellis at the corner of the house.

"Where are we going, Mama?" Fear echoed in the child's voice, but he mirrored her actions, and she couldn't be more proud of him.

"To the rooftop. We'll be safer there than on the ledge." God, she hoped that were true. In the darkness, it was difficult to see, and with her skirting that kept being caught beneath her feet, it would prove a miracle if she didn't fall. Already, trying to cling to the brickwork had resulted in two broken fingernails and hopelessly snagged clothing, but what was that compared with their lives?

"This is an adventure!"

"I'm glad you think so." Fear sat heavy in her throat she wanted to retch from it. Panic continued to fill her chest, pushed her past the point of all reason, but she refused to think about it.

Finally, there was no more ledge, and to gain the rooftop, she would need to take a leap of faith and jump three feet. Looking at her son, seeing the absolute trust in his little face, she swallowed the worst of her fears. "We need to jump. Can you do it?"

"Yes." Jacob nudged her hip with a hand. "You can too, Mama. To be away from here and that man who took me."

Oh, dear. As much as she'd hoped he hadn't been aware of what was going on, her son was intelligent enough to glean some knowledge. "Here we go." Thinking about Hudson and how he was giving her the time she needed to affect an escape, Theodosia pushed off from the ledge and jumped. Landing on the terra cotta tiles with dignity wasn't an option, and she half-rolled half-slid to a halt on the flat roof. Her knees and hands ached, but at least she hadn't broken anything. "Your turn." She gestured to the boy. "As quietly as you can."

With a sound suspiciously like a giggle, the boy followed her lead. He landed in a crouch as if he were made for this type of play. "That was bully fun."

Her heart pounded so hard she could only nod. "We still have a long way to go until the danger has passed." Fisting her skirting, Theodosia carefully picked her way across the rounded tiles. One of them cracked and skittered out from beneath the sole of her slipper. She involuntarily screamed as she fought for purchase but eventually, she found her balance and continued on, and still her pulse pounded hard through her veins.

Finally, they reached the corner of the villa where the wooden trellis reached up but only for two stories. She would need to lower herself off the roof in order to get a foothold in the vines. The task frightened her down to her soul, but it was the only way. "We're going to climb down to the ground."

"I have always wanted to do something like this." Still thinking of their escape as an adventure, the boy went ahead of her. "I'll show you how."

Theodosia nodded. "Be careful." When he disappeared beneath the slight overhang of the roof, her heart went into her throat, then a little white hand waved.

"Come on, Mama. It's fun."

"Your definition of that word is vastly different from mine." Saying a prayer and hoping for the best, she dropped to her knees and put her back to the sky. Then she lowered first one leg, and finding a foothold with her toes, testing the weight, she balanced on her stomach and put the other leg down until that foot, too, rested securely in the vines twisted through the trellis.

The sound of fabric ripping met her ears as she made the same movement again and again until she gripped the wooden trellis with her hands. A pungent scent of greenery mixed with the cloying aromas of night-blooming flowers as she continued to climb down, but then she made the mistake of checking her position. The ground seemed to rush up at her, and she wondered if she'd survive a fall from two stories up.

Darkness shimmered at the edges of her vision. With a gasp, she clutched at the vines and the wood of the trellis. "Oh, God." *Please don't let me faint now!* Severe fright overtook her so that she shook from it, nearly frozen, somewhere between the second and third floors. "I cannot do this."

"Mama, you must." Jacob touched her ankle, and she almost screamed from the unexpected contact. "We need to get away from the bad men. I don't want to go to England with them."

That spurred her into action. As if she had steel in her spine, Theodosia forced herself to relax and ignore the fear. She nodded, took a deep breath. "Right." Her job was to find safety for herself and her son. Hudson would join them as soon as he could. She hoped.

And once more, she found footholds and notches to grasp with her hands as she climbed down, down, down.

By the time Theodosia reached the ground at the rear of the villa, she shook from nerves and fear, but the moment Jacob wrapped his arms about her waist and hugged her, some of that faded. It had all been worth it. They were safe.

"Come. We need to run, though the gardens preferably," she told her son as she took his hand.

Click!

The unmistakable sound of a pistol cocking sent ice into her blood. "I rather think that won't be possible."

Slowly, as her stomach protested, Theodosia turned. Hanneford had leveled the nose of the pistol at her. "This ends tonight, Lady Ballantyne. The boy belongs with me."

Oh, dear God.

Chapter Fifteen

Winded, hurting, and exhausted, Hudson threw a final punch and his second assailant finally fell to the floor with a rather loud thud.

He shook out his right hand with its busted and bloody knuckles and rushed to the window. *Shit.* From his vantage point, he spied Theodosia in her golden gown with the moonlight winking off the beadwork standing in front of the dark form of a man, and he'd wager the contents of his bank account it was the marquess holding her a gun point. Why else wouldn't she have taken her son and run away? His gaze jogged to the smaller, darker form behind her which had to be Jacob. Yes, they'd hit into a snag.

It would take too much time to run through the corridors of the villa and the stairs to exit the house, so he climbed out the same window where the woman he loved had affected her escape. Only to land into more dire straits.

Damn, damn, damn.

Then his respect and admiration for her rose when he encountered the stone ledge just below the window. How she'd managed to make her way to the roof without fainting, he had no idea, but the fact that she had impressed the hell out of him.

When he jumped onto the roof, a few of the terra cotta tiles gave way beneath him. He scrabbled to keep his balance and once he did, Hudson continued onward. Where had she gone from here? There was literally nothing there and he frowned into the darkness. Then he saw the trailing vines that went up the rear of the villa. Carefully making his way to the edge of the roof, a quick glance downward showed a trellis covered in vines, greenery, and flowers. The sharp scent of recently disturbed and crushed plant life met his nose and betrayed the passage of someone before him.

They'd gone this way.

As he attempted to dangle his body over the side of the roof to access the trellis, he nearly plunged to his doom when one of the tiles came away in his hand. Though he hung onto the roof by one hand with all the muscles in his body aching, he finally found purchase in the vines with the toes of his boots and breathed a sigh of relief.

The first thing he would do when he was back in Theodosia's company was to kiss the hell out of her as well as bundle her safely into his arms, but then would ask her to never do something as dangerous as that again, for his heart couldn't take it.

With more speed than finesse, Hudson made his way down the side of the villa, crashing through the greenery and breaking more than a few rungs on the trellis as he went. The second the soles of his boots met the grass, he breathed out a sigh and then took off at a run in the direction he'd last glimpsed Theodosia and her son, but he plunged into the back gardens. The trees and shrubberies would keep him hidden until the time came to attack the marquess and take him into custody.

The closer he came to the spot where the marquess held Theodosia at gunpoint, the more conversation reached his ears. Of course the man was talking. Hudson rolled his eyes as he crept forward as quietly as he could. Villains adored hearing their own plans, loved telling others how clever they thought they were. He kept to the shadows and the high hedges as the marquess marched them down a pathway that ran parallel to the gardens. Eventually, it would lead to the wall at the rear of the property, and there was no doubt a closed carriage waiting on the street to carry the boy away, for Hanneford had no need of Theodosia.

"Did you truly think I didn't know what you and Ballantyne did that night? I have eyes everywhere, and not only in London." The man didn't bother to hide the contempt for her in his voice.

She whimpered when the marquess prodded her shoulder with the nose of the pistol. "At least we weren't about to commit murder."

Hudson feared for the boy. He would be confused by this conversation, perhaps even disturbed from such candid talk for a long time following.

A bark of laughter came from Hanneford. "Neither was I. That was the maid's task."

"No doubt you would have seen to it that Doris had a terrible accident shortly after she returned from the park."

"Perhaps." It didn't sound as if the marquess cared much either way. But then, a man without morals wouldn't. "I had too many bastards as it was, and most of them girls which I have no use for, but it was a busy time, and I was under heavy pressure in parliament. I told that maid to take of the baby."

"Which she did," Theodosia was quick to point out, which earned her a hit to her temple with the butt of the marquess' pistol. With a cry, she stumbled to her knees.

The boy uttered a frightened exhalation of alarm.

From his hiding spot, Hudson tamped on a growl. The man would pay for that. Just when he would have revealed his presence, she struggled to her feet and glared at Hanneford.

"Intimidation and physical violence are the only way you can be heard." She tsked her tongue and shook her head. "I pity you."

"And I have the same for you, so desperate for a child that you would steal one." He waved the pistol, but she refused to turn about. "Everything would have been fine except you and your too-noble husband had to take the maid in, save her life along with the boy's, thus making this into a bigger issue that I now have to dirty my hands with."

"Poor thing."

From behind the shrubberies, Hudson quietly cheered her on. Theodosia's bravery in the face of certain death was astounding. As of yet, she still had the situation well in hand.

She propped her hands on her hips, and at this close distance, Hudson discerned tears and rips in her once beautiful gown, made sure Jacob stayed behind her. Damn, she would use her body as a shield for her child. Not that it would help, for the marquess would shoot her and take the boy, regardless. Where the devil had she lost an angel wing? The other one was bent and mangled.

"You didn't want the boy eight years ago, but Nathaniel and I did. The babe had been clearly abandoned; Doris even confirmed it as well as her orders." Fury shook in her voice. The disgust in her expression evident in the moonlight. "Once a person leaves a child out in the elements to die, that's the end of it. We were well within our rights to take him."

"You stole him." The marquess didn't relax his grip on the pistol. It remained steady on her heart.

"No, I *loved* him, where you viewed him only as an inconvenience." She patted Jacob's hand and pushed him once more behind her. "He thrived with me; he is *my* son as sure as if I birthed him."

"How pathetic can you be, Lady Ballantyne? You have twisted the truth. I'm told finding oneself barren often warps the mind."

Oh, dear God. Hudson hated the marquess in that moment. Deliberately taunting a woman over her reproduction status was the height of detestable.

A muffled sob came from Theodosia. "I found a way, Hanneford, and I will die defending *my* son."

"Mama?" So much fright rode in that lone word that Hudson's heart squeezed.

Hanneford scoffed. "Such a touching scene, and no doubt it will come to pass. The child is mine, and you have no claim. You are a criminal."

"No. I raised him; *you* threw him out like rubbish. Which one of is right do you think?

Which one of us truly broke the law?" Tears wove through her question.

"You did." There was a growl in the marquess' voice. "I have a higher rank than you, and if you survive this night, I will take great pleasure in crushing you into dust, Lady Ballantyne."

She shook her head while Jacob buried his face in her skirting. "Why do you want him now? What had transpired to change your mind? As you said, you have many bastards."

The inquiry apparently took Hanneford by surprise, for he chuckled, and a brief smile curved his mouth as if he relished telling an additional tale. "My wife died a few years back, in childbirth. She never could carry a child to full term, and all of those births would have resulted in sons."

"Then it's true. You need an heir."

"I do."

"And you've no doubt put forth the story that your eldest has been away at an obscure relative's estate this whole time for his health or whatnot, and you have just recalled him back to London so he can learn how to be the marquess."

"How clever you are, Lady Ballantyne. Impressive." He kept the pistol trained on her while his eyes flashed like a snake's might in the moonlight. "Yes, I need an heir; young Jacob here will do well with me, I think."

"To learn all your horrible secrets? To be made in your image of a true villain?" Her voice went up an octave with each question.

"That remains to be seen and is no longer your concern." He gestured with the gun. "Move. There is a carriage waiting for you. In three hours, news will come back to Rome of a tragic accident. It was after midnight, the driver was drunk, and you, unfortunately, were innocently killed."

"No." Theodosia curled her hands into fists and held them at the ready as if the dear woman would pummel him into the ground. "You will *not* touch my son unless I'm dead."

The marquess snorted as if that were quite the joke. "That is my original plan, and exactly what I doled out to your husband when we had very much this same conversation."

Oh, God. Behind the hedges, Hudson gawked. She now had confirmation the marquess had ordered her husband's murder. The man was insane. Then and there, he vowed he would do everything in his power to see the lord in prison.

"You blackhearted louse! My husband was worth twelve of you; many men are, but now you will feel my wrath for what you've done to my family!" Theodosia stepped aside and shoved Jacob. "Run. Follow the gardens."

The child's eyes were wide with fright. "But Mama—"

She pushed him again, kept her body between the boy and the marquess. "Don't argue with! Run and don't stop running until I come for you. Do you understand?"

"Yes." Then the boy was off, shoving his way through the high hedges and then pelting down the darkened paths. He zipped past Hudson, his little legs pumping.

"Shit." Hudson was faced with making an agonizing decision. Did he stay and rescue Theodosia or catch up to her son and keep him safe? The one absolute was clear: Jacob couldn't go with the marquess.

Cursing softly while the sounds of a physical struggle drifted to his ears — obviously Theodosia had engaged the enemy — he ran as silently as he could after the boy. He was her legacy and her son, the most valuable thing in her life. At a fork in the path, the boy paused, searching this way and that, so Hudson came up behind him and dropped a gentle hand upon the slight shoulder.

"Argh!" Jacob whipped about and drilled a little fist into Hudson's belly. "No! Leave me alone!"

Pain blossomed through his gut and reactivated all the other aches and pains within his body. He gasped for breath but once more put his hand on the boy's shoulder. "Hold, Jacob." The command was wheezy. "I'm a friend of your mother's."

The boy flailed, tried to tear himself away. "That is what the marquess said." He continued to struggle. "He is *not* nice."

"No, he is not."

"Will he kill my mama?" So much worry wove through the inquiry that Hudson's heart squeezed in sympathy.

"Not while I'm around." With a grunt of pain, he kneeled before the boy, ignoring the small pieces of gravel that dug into his knee. "My name is Hudson Ridley. I was tasked by your mother to find you and bring you back to her. I used to work with Bow Street."

"An inspector," he breathed with awe. Though he was halfway between fight and flight, he paused and stared into Hudson's face. "Mama is in trouble."

"I know." Every moment they lingered there could see her in further jeopardy. "Will you help me fight the villain and rescue her?"

The boy nodded. "Then might we go home?"

Hudson's heart lurched so hard he feared it might break into two. "To England?"

"No, to Uncle Thomas' house. I miss my friends and my toys." He glanced over Hudson's shoulder. "The bad man said I was his son. Is that true?"

Oh, God. Hudson's heart tugged for an entirely different reason. It was not his place to have this talk. "Of course not." He met the child's eyes without a flinch. "That man is a said, horrid liar who is mean to everyone he's ever met. You are your *mama's* son, and your papa was *very* brave, even at the last."

God, please let that be true and let this child believe me.

Finally, the boy nodded. With tears sparkling in his eyes, he said, "Let's go rescue Mama."

"Good. A fine man you'll be later in life, I think." With a range of emotion clogging his chest, Hudson stood. He ignored the pain. There would be time for that later. "Your mama is brave too, but she might need help." Worry for Theodosia pulsed through his blood with every step that he took.

"I will be brave too," Jacob said in a tiny voice.

"I have no doubts." As they crept back along the garden path where he'd last seen Theodosia, the boy snuck his hand into Hudson's. The touch of that little hand in his caused his heart to swell in ways he hadn't anticipated.

So close yet so far from a buried, life-long dream, but now was not the time to ponder if it was something he could yet grasp.

I won't fail you, Dia.

He couldn't. There was no other option.

By the time he and Jacob reached the spot where he left her fighting with the marquess, the sounds of a struggle increased. "Stay here," he told the boy. "Keep to the hedges until I can overpower him and it's safe."

"All right." Jacob nodded. He tugged on Hudson's hand. "You *will* rescue her, right?"

"I promise she'll be safe." Hudson once more peered at the scene from the hedges.

Somehow, Theodosia had procured a large, thick tree branch, and from the looks of things, she'd gotten in a few hits to the marquess. Why hadn't Hanneford fired the pistol? As he glanced about the area, the moonlight glinted off the barrel of the weapon as it lay a few feet away from them in the grass. It seemed the marvelous woman had knocked the weapon from his hand!

Grunts and cries of pain filled the air and redirected his attention. At his side, Jacob whimpered. He patted the little back and then nearly tore through the hedges when she took a blow from the man's fist, but she lashed out with a sideways kick that landed squarely in the marquess' gut. Where had she learned to fight like that?

Hanneford uttered a roar of rage. He bent over as if he were in pain, but instead of catching his breath, he charged at her. His shoulder connected with Theodosia's chest and they both fell hard to the ground.

Jacob attempted to stifle his crying with a hand over his mouth.

Poor lad. "It will all be right as rain. You'll see." Hudson ruffled the boy's hair. "Stay here." Then he crept from the shrubberies and was immediately tackled by a man approaching the scene at run—one of the men he'd previously fought in the house.

As quickly as he could and while in copious amounts of pain, he struggled into a standing position, and was obliged to duck a blow. Completely out of patience with the whole scene, Hudson swung out with his fist, connecting with the other man's jaw. The man merely stumbled back a few steps. "Why won't you stay knocked out?"

His opponent grunted and gave him a gap-toothed grin.

While the sounds of Theodosia's fight with the marquess fell upon his ears, Hudson again dodged a blow and when he gave another, the man danced away. Quick to recover, the other man delivered an upper cut jab to Hudson's chin. His teeth crashed together and there was enough force in the punch to send him reeling. He went down hard and landed on his back, winded and fighting off pain that had blackness flirting with the edges of his vision.

There was no time to give in to such weakness.

As his opponent advanced and the sounds of fighting reached his ears from Theodosia's direction, Hudson staggered to his feet and pulled his knife from his boot. Slashing at the other man didn't result in anything, for he easily evaded the blade. Narrowly ducking his next punch, he delivered one of his own, but his adversary merely grunted.

"Enough. If you want me that badly, come at me. I've grown tired of this." In more ways than one.

So, he did.

"Mr. Ridley, watch out!"

Obviously, the boy was watching from behind the hedges. With a nod, Hudson kept his gaze on the approaching man then threw his knife. The moonlight danced on steel. Seconds later, the blade lodged in the man's chest, hilt deep. His opponent grunted. A look of surprise crossed his face and he paused. Finally, he fell to the ground and this time he didn't get up.

"Oh, thank God." Exhaustion sank into his bones. He was almost dead on his feet, but before he could decide on what to do next, life paused around him for a few dreadful moments.

Bang!

The pistol report echoed in the silence of the night.

With his heart in his throat, Hudson swung around to assess the situation. Theodosia screamed, and the hairs on his nape prickled. Then she crumpled to the ground while a curl of smoke rose from the nose of Hanneford's pistol as he dangled the weapon at his side.

Somehow, the marquess had gotten hold of the damned gun and now he'd shot Theodosia.

"No!" Hudson bellowed with rage. A red film dropped in front of his vision while his heart lurched, and life shuddered back into real time. "You fucking, piece of rubbish!" He flew at the marquess, catching him unawares from the back, relieved him of the pistol and then proceeded to beat the hell out of the man with the butt until Hanneford slumped unconscious to the ground.

As fear turned his blood to ice, he dropped the pistol and rushed to Theodosia's side. "Please don't be dead," he whispered as he knelt close to her. "Please." Gently, carefully, he rolled her onto her back. "Theodosia?"

With a quick glance to the hedges where he'd left Jacob and seeing no sign of the boy, Hudson turned his attention back to the woman lying on the grass. His heart had lodged in his throat, for she was far too still. Knots invaded his stomach, pulling tight. In considerable pain, he leaned over her, couldn't lose her. "Dia, please don't leave me. I need you." Quickly, he checked for the gunshot wound, to see the damage, but there was oddly no blood marring the bodice of her gown.

What the devil was this? He stared and frowned.

No blood.

"What the hell?" With hope rising in his tight chest, Hudson examined her belly, her chest, her shoulders, her sides, but there were no holes in the gown's fabric. How was that possible? He slipped his gloved fingers to her chest, examined the low bodice of the gown. Aside from tears and snags from her adventure, there was no blood. But he kept going. *Ah, there.* A red welt was forming beneath the necklace she wore. Then he sucked in a breath. A ball was securely lodged in the gold of the ornamental circlet. She had been saved by the slim margin of an inch.

"Thank the lord." Almost giddy with relief, Hudson clutched Theodosia's hand and rested his ear over her chest in an effort to listen to her pulse. When that faint rhythm was detected, he couldn't help but sob with gratitude. Once the tears started, it was difficult to stem the tide, so he waited out the emotions.

A minute, a few, an hour—a lifetime— later, he became aware of pressure on his fingers from where she squeezed them. As he lifted his head away, she touched the side of his face, traced the scars on his cheek. "I do not think now is an appropriate time to try and seduce me," she joked in a whisper. When she laughed, the sound quickly turned into a moan of pain. "My chest hurts."

"I'll wager it does." Beside himself with happiness, he couldn't give her more words.

Was completely incapable of it. Instead, Hudson gently gathered her into his arms and then kissed her, told her by his actions how he felt about her in this moment and all the rest. She clung to his shirt and kissed him back, and it was the sweetest gift he'd ever been given.

"Mama!" Jacob's shout interrupted the embrace as he ran out of the garden. As Theodosia pulled away from Hudson, she caught her son in her arms. "Mama, I'm hungry," he said without preamble. "Might we have some of that Roman pizza I like?"

Both Hudson and Theodosia broke out into laughter. It was a much-needed tension breaker. She hugged the boy tight. "Of course." Then she leaned over and practically fell into his waiting arms. "My dear Mr. Ridley, I believe I would like to go home. I'm rather done with tonight, so could you please escort us there?"

"It would be my great honor." And if fate was kind, this wouldn't be the last time that he saw her, because he couldn't fathom living the remainder of his life without her.

Chapter Sixteen

May 11, 1818
Minerva Villa
Rome

Theodosia awoke to a plethora of aches and pains in every part of her body. Late morning sunlight streamed through opened windows of her bedchamber. Obviously, Doris had pulled back the draperies in an effort to encourage her awake. With a half-stifled moan, she turned onto her side as her mind revisited the events that had happened since she'd returned home the night she'd fought with Hanneford.

Oh, Hudson had been magnificent! As they exited the hired carriage, her strength gave out, so he'd bundled her up into his arms and had carried her inside the house. Since her brother was still attending his society event, the staff had buzzed around them, exclaimed over the return of her son, and the former Bow Street man had carried her upstairs and laid her on her bed.

After that, things were a bit of a blur, but he'd left with promises to check on her. She must have passed out after Doris had presided over a bath, and she'd slept most of yesterday. Jacob hadn't left her side and had slept next to her, but he hadn't done that last night. In fact, her son had fled to his own room earlier that morning to play with his toy soldiers. Everyone in the house pandered to his requests, and he was never left alone, leaving her the freedom to rest.

She hadn't minded, for her body needed time to heal, but she fretted that she hadn't seen Hudson. On the one hand, she was beyond grateful to be alive and have her son back, but on the other hand, she was worried and felt an unfathomable loss deep in her soul.

Had Hudson considered the case closed and had returned to his life before he'd met her?

The longcase clock in the corridor outside her rooms chimed the eleventh hour. Seconds later, Doris bustled into the room with a breakfast tray.

"It's good to see you awake. I thought you would sleep for days." The cheerful tone of her voice made Theodosia smile as she set the tray on the bed beside her. "Tea or coffee?"

"Tea." What did Hudson drink upon awakening in the morning? Did he sleep in a nightshirt or in the nude? The urge to see him grew overwhelming. "But I'll have it while dressing. I don't wish to waste more time." Her cuts and bruises ached like the devil as she slipped out of bed and then went behind the privacy screen to attend to necessary things.

"Are you sure you wish to dress, my lady? You should stay in bed all day." Doubt rang in the maid's voice. "Those bruises must pain you."

"Oh, they do, but I refuse to lie around like an invalid." Dressing was a painful endeavor, for it required her to move her body, but she got through the process with minimal complaints. The gown of robin's egg blue was a pretty splash of much needed color, and it immediately lifted her spirits. She directed Doris into putting her hair into a simple chignon and then took a few sips of tea. "Where is the ambassador this morning."

"In the drawing room. He refuses to leave the house right now with you recovering and the boy under the roof." Doris shrugged. "In fact, for the past day or so, he has conducted his meetings in his study."

"He must feel guilty." Yet Theodosia was impressed with her brother's commitment. As she sipped her tea, she said, "Have there been visitors?"

A sly look seeped into the maid's expression. "Do you mean has a certain large, mysterious investigator called for you?"

Heat jumped into her cheeks. "Well? Has he?" There was no sense dancing about it.

"Mr. Ridley sent a lovely floral bouquet yesterday. It's in your sitting room. He did come by yesterday evening, but Ambassador Wetherington turned him out."

"What?" Her heart constricted. "Why?"

"I would have no idea, my lady."

Hudson had come to check on her and her brother wouldn't let him see her. Annoyance stabbed into her chest. "Never mind. I will take care of it." Quickly, she finished her tea but ignored the toast and jam. Her appetite had fled, and until she'd settled her future, she wouldn't be able to eat. "Please look after Jacob in the event I need to abruptly visit Mr. Ridley."

The maid's eyebrows soared. "Oh?"

Another round of heat infused her cheeks as she hunted for the matching slippers for the gown. "Do hush, Doris."

The other woman giggled. "You love him, my lady."

As she slipped a foot into a slipper, Theodosia smiled. "I suppose I do." There was no sense in denying it, for there was only one reason for the way she felt. With a peek into the cheval glass, she smoothed a hand over the front of the gown. The cuts and bruises that marred her skin were chilling, indeed, and it appeared as if she'd been beaten within an inch of her life, but she had saved her child and that was what mattered. "This bodice doesn't cover much." The bruised welt from where the ball had been stopped by the necklace was especially hideous.

"Wear the gown anyway. You were very brave."

"Perhaps I was." It still humbled her that the gift Nathaniel had given her had ended up saving her life. *If you are looking down at me, I thank you, and I hope you will be happy for me if I wish to move forward.* "Oh, Doris, a dog's breakfast probably looks better than I do right now." There was no hiding the marks on her face.

"My lady, Mr. Ridley won't care. He no doubt loves you to distraction already."

"I don't know." It was too soon. Impossible, really, wasn't it? But having that hope made her heart beat a bit faster. With a frown, she turned away from the mirror. "I will strive to do the best I can. Whatever the outcome of our conversation, life still goes on."

But why couldn't it do that with him?

"I hope you have good fortune, my lady, but I think that you will." Doris' smile was wide. "You deserve every happiness."

"Thank you." She left her room and went directly to the drawing room to search out her brother. As soon as she entered, she said, "We should talk, brother."

Thomas glanced up from his scrutiny of a sheaf of papers. "You should be in bed, resting. You have had a rather horrid time of it, from what I've been able to glean from Jacob."

Ah, so he'd been questioning her son, had he? If that were true, then he had also learned she and Hudson had kissed that night after everything. Well, there was nothing for it, and she certainly wouldn't apologize. "I will decide what I should do or what is best for me."

He sighed and set the paperwork on the cushion beside him. "Meaning?"

Theodosia shook her head. "Doris said you turned Hudson away yesterday when he came to call. Why?"

"Straight to it, hmm?" Thomas huffed with apparent aggravation. "The man wished to pay his addresses, had asked me before you apparently did battle with a marquess, but I feel he is not good enough for you, so I refused his request and hinted that he have no more contact with you after the case concluded."

"What?" With her knees suddenly having the strength of cooked porridge, she quickly sat on a chair near to his location. Hudson had asked permission to pay his addresses? Warmth trickled into her tight chest. That had to mean something. "And you never thought to tell me?"

He shrugged. "There was no reason to."

"There was every reason!" Butterflies danced through her lower belly as she sprang up from her chair. "I need to see him."

"You are in no condition to go visiting." His voice was hard as he stood. "And I will not let you go to that man's lodging house, especially unaccompanied."

She huffed at his highhandedness, wished to shock him. "If I am fortunate, more than mere visiting will occur." A grin tugged at the corners of her mouth when his eyes widened, and color crept over his cravat. "I know my own mind, Thomas. I am quite capable of living my own life; haven't I proved that after what happened two days ago?" When he didn't answer, she sighed. "I… I think I'm in love with Mr. Ridley."

"Think clearly, Theodosia. He is not worthy of you, and you can certainly do better than him." He crossed his arms at his chest. "Love is a fleeting emotion. You must think of your future. Of Jacob's future."

For the first time she saw her brother not as her sibling but as a man who had been hurt — flat out gutted, really — by love that didn't last. Rarely did he talk about that dark time, but she hadn't known it had affected him so deeply. "Thomas, listen to me." She laid a hand on his arm, urged him to relax his closed-off stance. "I am thinking more clearly now than I have for years. No longer am I lost or alone."

"What does that mean?" He clasped his hands behind his back. No more did anger go through his expression.

Cool relief swept through her. "Mr. Ridley—Hudson—makes me feel wanted and needed as if I matter as a woman."

"Of course you do."

She rolled her eyes. "Oh, stop. You don't see me, the *real* me, Thomas. I am but an additional responsibility you don't want. You think me weak and retiring or an object that needs protected."

"Because you are valuable to me," he admitted in a low voice.

"Hush, then, and let me speak from the heart." Theodosia met his eyes, implored him understand. "What I have found with Hudson is surprising. He brings out the best in me, pushes me to be... more, and do you know what? I do the same for him. Do we clash, sometimes, with our opinions? Oh, yes, but isn't that what makes life exciting?"

"Ha. There is more to love than that. It cuts deep, disappoints just as much, destroys a person from the inside out until there is nothing left." A certain amount of bitterness wove through his voice.

"You poor thing." She squeezed his hand. "I hope you discover that isn't the only truth, Thomas." As she pondered her next words, Theodosia moved away from him. "As I told you a few days ago, I am ready for a change, to live again. I believe I can do that with Hudson."

"Why him?"

"Why not him? He is everything kind and protective and honorable." A sigh escaped her. "I don't wish to be frightened any longer of Hanneford." She'd had to confess all to Thomas when he returned home that night and found her beaten and bloodied in her bed.

"I agree with you on that point."

She nodded. "Hudson protects me."

"I'm trying to protect you!"

"No, you are keeping me a prisoner surrounded by pretty things and useless gentlemen who have no depth. Hudson sets my fears to rest, believes in me so that I might fight my own battles. No one has ever done that for me. Not even Nathaniel, and you know how much I loved him."

"Everyone fails the people they love."

"That is why love is so wonderfully confusing, but it also encompasses everything. It forgives." Theodosia offered him a tiny smile. "I am sorry you didn't have that."

Thomas tugged on the knot of his cravat. "But this man isn't—"

"No. This conversation is over." She pressed her hands to burning cheeks. "If he will still have me, I want him. I think I've been waiting for someone like him ever since I came to Rome." With a hand on her heart, she gave him a genuine smile. "Now I know what real breathlessness feels like instead of how I cannot breathe in London's polluted air. It's what I experience every time I see him. It's wonderful."

"But, can he take care of you?"

"I am eager to find out because that is also a part of love. The discovery. Together." She couldn't stop smiling as excitement buzzed at the base of her spine. "It will be so much fun, and I cannot wait for Jacob to come to know him as well."

"Please, Theo, listen to me." Thomas took a step toward her, but she shook her head.

"Don't worry. All is well. I should return in a few hours." All she wanted was to see Hudson, to reassure herself he hadn't been severely hurt in those fights.

"But love doesn't happen in a day! It's impossible to think so. Irresponsible, even."

Oh, how many times had she thought that herself? "There are times when I think love can be anything it wishes; it certainly affects people in different ways. Who are we to say what is the right or what is the wrong way to love?" She stared at him, and he stared back, his jaw working but no words forthcoming. "Wish me well, brother dear, or else you will lose me and my son." On this she was quite confident. Her life was her own; it was time to start living it again.

His swallow was audible. There was a certain wistfulness in his eyes as he looked at her. "Are you happy?"

"Very much so."

Finally, Thomas nodded. "Then I will voice no more objections. Unless he is horrid to you. Then I will call him out."

A giggle welled within her. She closed the distance between them and then bussed his cheek. "Hudson is not that sort of man." With a wave, she fairly danced across the room to the door. "I will be back soon. If Jacob asks for me, tell him I've gone out to ask Mr. Ridley to dinner."

"At least take a bonnet and gloves! Since you've been in Rome, you've grown too scandalous," her brother groused.

"It's too late for all that, and besides, skirting society has rather become habit." She winked at her sibling. "I'm not that Diamond of the First Water any longer, thank goodness." Until Jacob grew and could take up the reins of his father's title, she had no need to be proper; having those bonds fall away was a wonderful thing.

As she walked the few streets over to his lodging house, her steps were light, but her heart raced. In mere moments, she would see him, would tell him what she'd wanted to say since that waltz at Hanneford's villa... since practically the moment she met him.

Upon gaining the entry hall and walking past Mrs. Claudian's sitting room, she waved to the landlady. That woman beamed and waved back.

"I will have tea ready for you when you are done, my lady," she assured Theodosia. "It is about time Mr. Ridley was domesticated."

"Indeed, it is, Mrs. Claudian, but I rather prefer him with that raw and ragged side." With a grin that couldn't be contained, Theodosia ran up the stairs until she stood at Hudson's door. Only then did doubts beset her. What if she was wrong? What if he'd only been kind and affectionate toward her because he felt sorry for her while working her case?

Shoving those doubts to the back of her mind, forgetting how scandalous it was to even be here to begin with, Theodosia rapped her knuckles upon the wooden panel. When there was no answer—verbal or otherwise—panic welled in her chest. She knocked again, this time with more urgency. It took an inordinate amount of time for him to come to the door, and once the panel swung open, she understood why.

Hideous purple and blue bruises decorated his face and chest, for he was only dressed in a pair of buff-colored breeches. No doubt his body hurt as hers did, but she couldn't help but devour his form with her eyes. Despite the battering he'd received, he was as solid as he'd ever been. That heavy mat of dark hair that spread out over his upper chest in an abstract butterfly pattern had her itching to touch him. Finally, she wrenched her attention back to his face. "You poor thing. I shouldn't have disturbed your rest." His hair, wild and unkempt, stood up on one side as if he'd slept hard just before she'd arrived.

"Theodosia." His expression filled with pleasure, and he raked his gaze up and down her person as she had just done to him. "No, no. Please, come in. Pardon my appearance. I wasn't expecting visitors, and the act of donning clothes hurt too much."

"Think nothing of it."

Quickly, he stood aside until she entered and then he quickly closed the door behind her. "You're the one who should be abed."

"Fear not. I plan to be there later today." Was that too bold?

A red flush went up his neck, unhidden due to the absence of proper clothing. "Ah." He led her into the drawing room at a slow pace while she admired his taut backside. "Are you well? You have as many bruises as I do."

She snorted. "I rather think you had the worst of it. At least your eye isn't swollen shut any longer." There was still a gaping hole where missing furniture should be, so she perched on the edge of a settee. "What became of the Marquess of Hanneford?"

"Before I escorted you home, I sent a footman to rouse the local polizia. When we left, they had him in custody. The morning after, I went by that office to interview him. He will be escorted back to England to serve trial for the murder of your husband, since he confessed to that crime. You and I both heard it."

The breath stalled in her lungs, and she gasped. "That would mean I'd need to testify. He could retaliate. Come after Jacob."

"*I* would do that in your stead." Hudson lowered himself gingerly into a chair near to her location. "However, when I told him he had no chance of staying out of prison and what life was like for inmates, he crumbled."

"What happened?"

"We struck a deal."

Another wave of panic welled in her chest. "He *won't* be put into prison?"

"He will not." When she became agitated, he held up a hand. "However, in order to do that, he is going to summon his solicitor to draw up paperwork. Basically, Hanneford has promised to write a draft to your bank in London and deposit into your account ten thousand pounds for the care, upkeep, and education of Jacob."

"What?" How was any of this possible?

Hudson nodded. "Beyond that, he will also sign a document giving up any and all claims—real or imagined—to the boy. Once that document is filed with the courts, Jacob will legally be your son as well as Nathaniel's if anyone cared to research, and no one can take him away from you again."

Tears welled in her eyes. "While I thank you for the diplomacy, how do I know the marquess will be bound by those papers? He's not exactly an upstanding citizen."

"Calm yourself." Amusement danced in his eyes. "I threatened him within an inch of his life." A grin tugged at the corners of his mouth. "As much as I want to see him in Newgate and then hung, men like Hanneford have a talent for paying off guards and officials, and very rarely do peers make it that far into the legal system." He shrugged. "I explained to him I've written to my contacts at Bow Street and have told them what he'd done. That the crime deserves constant surveillance by any number of their men."

"Did he believe you?" She could hardly dare breathe.

"He seemed frightened enough. I rather doubt his acts against you and your family are the only ones he's guilty of, so this must have made an impression."

"Did you truly write to Bow Street?"

"I did."

"And did he truly write to his solicitor?"

"He did. I witnessed the act and then read the letter. Both of them. They were posted this morning." His expression turned serious. "The man won't bother you again. You needn't fear for Jacob's future. As for Hanneford, he will remain in the custody of the local polizia until he's to board the ship returning to England on the fifteenth, and he is barred from coming into Rome for the remainder of his life."

Theodosia stared at him in shock. "How did you manage that?" She pressed a hand to her heart, willed it to stop beating so fast. "I cannot fathom how much effort it took."

"There is no end to what I would do for you, Dia. However, I didn't do it all on my own."

"Oh?" Why couldn't she breathe properly?

He nodded. "Your brother assisted. He has a knack for contracts, and the diplomacy aspect was his touch. I simply wanted to beat the marquess until he agreed."

She gawked at him as if she'd never seen him before. "What do you mean? Before I left today, he was quite stubborn about my claim that I needed to see you..." Well, she couldn't very well blurt out what she felt.

"I don't doubt it." Another half grin curved his lips. "We have had many conversations since he first rejected my earlier request this week to pay my addresses. I think by doing this, the ambassador was trying to apologize and agree to my suit."

Sandra Sookoo

"But…" Slowly, she shook her head. "But he still refused… He continued to argue with me…" His emotions regarding love had been all too real. "I'm confused."

Hudson snorted. With a groan, he stood up from his chair and relocated to a cushion beside her on the settee. "Perhaps I should explain."

Chapter Seventeen

The time had come for Hudson to tell her the contents of his heart. For better or for worse, he wanted Theodosia to know everything that he felt, and she could do what she would with the information, but for the first time in his life, he had the opportunity to do so.

He turned to her, breathed in the lilac scent she wore. *Dear God*, she was beautiful even with her face, arms, and chest decorated with bruises and scratches. Knowing Hanneford had given the worst of those injuries to her had made him want to pummel the man unconscious, but it had been Thomas who'd talked sense into him, who'd told him doing so would make him as hideous as the marquess. So, instead, they'd gotten revenge in the way of a gentleman.

"How does Jacob fare?"

Her expression changed from confusion and worry to relief. "He is well and doing what little boys do. Thank you for asking."

"From the tiny interaction I had with him two days ago, he seems to be a congenial boy with much potential." Unable to be so close to her without touching, Hudson took one of her hands in his. "Saving him, protecting him, seeing him with you only solidified my decision."

"It did?" Those gray-blue eyes of her never left his face, and from how desperately she clutched his hand, there were things she obviously needed to hear, perhaps say. "I'm afraid I was consumed with giving the marquess his just desserts."

"And you did it so well, sweeting." He brought her hand to his lips and placed a kiss on her middle knuckle. "You are fierce and determined, and I can't imagine a life without you in it in some capacity." Truly, there was no sense in skirting about the issue. "Even though I met you three days ago, it feels as if we have already been through a lifetime together."

"Well, in our defense, this case has been exceptionally intense."

"It has and thank the heavens it has come to a satisfying conclusion." He blew out a breath. "I'll admit, I had my doubts, but as it unfolded things began to make sense and we pushed through."

"And now?" Those two words were breathless, as if she were waiting for something.

Oh, she would forever keep him on his toes, push him to being better, and he couldn't think of anything better. "Now, I want to be more to you than the man who assisted in the effort of bringing your son home."

Theodosia's hand trembled in his. "You do?"

"I do." Needing more contact with her, Hudson released her hand in order to cup her cheek. "Nothing of this sort has ever happened to me, and I find myself discombobulated and discomfited by turns, but I'm also hopeful and excited." He shook his head, for this was an extraordinary thing. "Meeting you, spending time with you, coming to know you better has completely upended my life in ways I could never anticipate."

"It has been rather curious yet wonderful."

"Indeed. Usually, I am a man of few words." The longer he held her gaze, the more he wanted to dive into those cool, inviting pools and never leave. "However, there are certain things I must say to you, words I have never uttered to anyone, and now they sit on the tip of my tongue."

Amusement lit her face. "Then you'd best tell me straightaway."

He nodded. "You, my dear, are the love that came into my life without warning, without fanfare. I truly believe you crept into my heart and took possession before I could protest."

A frown tugged at the corners of her kissable lips. "*Do* you wish to? Protest, that is?"

"Absolutely not." Feeling rather mischievous, he plucked the few pins from her hair and when her hair fell about her shoulders in a blonde waterfall, a sigh shuddered from him. "Theodosia, despite the short physical time we have spent together, I feel as if I've known you—loved you—for a lifetime, and that I wish for you to know that I do, indeed, love you. The fact that it happened so suddenly and without warning has no bearing, for the fact remains that those feelings are there and quite real."

The look of joy that had come over her completely transformed her into the angel she'd pretended to be the night of the masquerade ball; he'd never seen her so beautiful as she was arrayed in love. "Oh, Hudson, that was so romantic."

His confidence faltered a bit. "While I agree, do you have something to say about that?" Was it vain of him to want to hear the words returned? After all, he had never been in this state before, had never met a woman with whom he'd admired so much that he wished to share his life with.

"You poor, lovely, dear man." Theodosia laid a palm to his cheek, traced the scars that marred his skin, and with every brush of her fingertips, he died a thousand deaths. Would this be the last time they shared such a moment? "I, too, have agonized over the swiftness and the intensity of the feelings I have for you."

"Does that mean—"

"Shh." She placed a finger over his lips, and he dared to take that digit into his mouth, suck on it, swirl his tongue about it while she watched him with round eyes and an expression that offered everything he'd ever wanted. "Oh." A blush stained her cheeks. All too adorable. "I think there are unique times when what someone feels is immediate and without rhyme or reason."

"This is true."

With a nod, Theodosia continued. "Two people share a glance from across a ballroom or they are thrown together like we were in extenuating circumstances. There's an overwhelming connection. When hands touch or skin brushes or tentative kisses are exchanged, those things only cement that connection, deepen it."

"What are you trying to say, sweeting?" Would she never come round to the point? But then, that was another thing he adored about her.

"Perhaps love doesn't need months or years to be figured out, to have it make sense. The heart always knows what is best; whether such love is right or wrong is anyone's guess, but the simple fact of being in love, of feeling that loveliness wrap around you is both startling and wonderful." She peered into his face and in that moment, there was no need for further conversation for the truth shone from her expression. "I have fallen in love with you, Hudson, and there is nowhere else I would rather be just now."

"Well, damn." His heart squeezed as it seemed to grow from being nurtured with hers. "I suspected, but hearing those words…" He forced a swallow into his suddenly dry throat. "They are so much sweeter than I could have anticipated."

"I am glad, for I will undoubtedly keep telling you." She threw herself into his arms and the press of her petal-soft mouth on his had the power to see him come undone.

For several seconds, he availed himself of her enthusiasm. The kiss changed to something frantic and heated, as it had the last time they were in this very room. He couldn't help himself as he dragged his lips down the side of her throat while cupping her breasts, teasing her nipples through the fabric of her gown. When her soft moans reached his ears, he resumed kissing her, and all too soon they were both breathless when they wrenched apart.

"Sweeting, hold." There was so much desire and stark need in her eyes that mirrored what was flowing through his veins that it took all his willpower not to carry her off to his bed. "Before we go any further, there is something I must ask."

"Oh, dear." The adorable woman put her hands to her cheeks. "You needn't."

"But I do." With another groan, Hudson slipped off the settee to rest on both knees before her. "We've known each other for three days. That cannot be helped, but I look forward to having a lifetime with you to discover your secrets and to reveal all of mine to you."

"Hudson…"

"What the future holds, I don't know, but together we'll meet it and give Jacob the best life a boy could ever ask for."

Then he left her only long enough to grab a small, red-linen box from a nearby table. As soon as he resumed his former position, he opened the box to reveal an oval-shaped opal whose colors gleamed and flashed within the milky background. After he'd had the talk with Hanneford along with Theodosia's brother, he'd come back to the lodging house and asked Mrs. Claudian to go shopping for an engagement ring with him. Buying such a bauble had removed a good chunk of coin from his account, but it was completely worth it to see the adoration in his Dia's eyes.

"Will you marry me?" Then his confidence faltered. "I realize I'm not considered a catch in society circles and I'm not the most attractive of men, and according to your brother I don't have an income that will keep you in style—"

"Yes." She met his gaze, and the love there nearly bowled him over. "Yes, I will marry you and be happy to do so. Nothing else matters, because you are exactly the man I need right now."

As Theodosia bounced her regard between the ring he still held and his face, everything became so clear. A wave of happiness and wonder pushed over her; never had she been more certain of anything in her life.

He peered at her in expectation. "Are you certain?"

"Oh, yes." She let him slip the ring onto the fourth finger of her left hand, where the light caught it and threw back rainbows. "I cannot think of anything I would rather do than marry you." Her voice caught, for there was so much emotion in her throat she wanted to both cry with joy and sob at being so frightened of this newfound happiness. "Jacob will be thrilled. He talks constantly about the investigator who fought with his bare fists in order to rescue his mother."

"I rather think you were well in control."

Even in this, he would remain humble regarding the part he'd played. "Come here, you adorable man." Needing so much more from him, Theodosia slipped her arms about his upper chest and claimed his lips. Oh, he felt so right in her arms, and she couldn't wait to have that solid mass of him pressed against her body.

The connection between them strengthened with each new kiss and caress. Desire quickly built infernos within her blood as she played her hands up and down his spine, explored the breadth of his shoulders, charted a course over the strong planes of his back and chest.

It took next to no time for Hudson to tug the bodice of her gown down. In his zeal, he might have torn the chemise beneath it, but Theodosia merely laughed; the raw power of him that would stop at nothing to possess her merely fanned the flames of her own passion. Then her breasts were in his large hands and when he worried the nipples into hardened, sensitive tips, need shuddered through her. She hooked a hand about his nape and encouraged him closer, crying out her pleasure when he took one of those buds into the warmth of his mouth.

Heat streaked through her body. Each time he played at her nipples, that heat increased until she fairly shook from it, wanted to share that with him. Hudson must have felt the same, for he left off with that exquisite form of torture to shove up her skirting. The roughness of the callouses on his palms added tantalizing friction everywhere he touched.

"Ah, Dia, never will I have enough of you." He gripped her hips, pulled her lower body to the edge of the settee, and then encouraged her thighs apart. "Shall I continue?"

"Must you ask?" Already, she'd sunk into a lethargic cloud as she lounged backward. "Give me everything you are."

"Always." With a cheeky grin, he buried his head between her thighs. The scrape of the stubble on his cheeks made her shiver with anticipation, but the second he encouraged the nubbin out of hiding at her center, she completely lost her grip on reality.

"Dear God." Struggling into a halfway upright position, Theodosia slipped the fingers of one hand into his hair, holding him close, guiding him to the spot she wanted him to be. "I cannot hold on… It's coming so fast…"

"Take all of it."

The warmth of his breath at her damp flesh, the reverberations of his voice, the friction from his fingers and tongue stole her away, caught her up in the spinning vortex of pleasure. Seconds later, a scream of repletion was ripped from her throat. Contractions rocked her core as release washed over her. For a few seconds, she floated on a wave where light and sound combined and temporarily removed her from the present.

When she came back to herself, she felt rather boneless, but a groan from him tugged a chuckle from her. "Shall I return the favor?"

"God, no, I won't be able to last, but just now, the thought of hauling myself off this floor seems all too painful." He sent her a wry glance. "I'm an old man."

"No, you are experienced." With a giggle, for her heart was as light as a feather, she joined him on the floor, encouraged him onto his back, and straddled his waist. "We shall commit to each other and this upcoming union on the floor. It matters not." She leaned over him and took shameless advantage of him as she kissed him.

His enthusiasm matched hers, and just like the last time they'd come together, heat engulfed them and suddenly kissing wasn't nearly enough. "Lift off a bit." Once she did as he asked, he quickly manipulated the buttons of his frontfalls. Then the gloriously hard, thick length of him was free, and she wasted no time in wrapping a hand about his member. "Careful, careful," he warned in a graveled voice. "I won't last."

"Perhaps I don't want you to, for I need this joining as much as you." The heady power she wielded in this position went straight to her head, and she smiled. "We are going to have a lovely time together, I think." Then she fit his tip to her opening, and as he gripped her hips and widened his legs, she lowered herself slowly, ever so slowly, onto his shaft until he fully filled her. Her eyelids fluttered as pleasure circled through her lower belly. "Oh, yes."

"Watching you is almost as potent as claiming you," he said in a broken whisper, and as he thrust upward, a wash of sensation flooded her. "I am so damned lucky."

"Yes, you are," she couldn't help but quip shortly before urgency guided her actions.

Now that she was engaged to this man and all of her doubts had been laid to rest, she was left with nothing except need and abandon. Without shame and enjoying every second of this coupling, Theodosia rode Hudson's shaft with varying degrees of speed and positioning. Depending on how she moved, friction rubbed over her swollen nubbin, hit a certain spot within her passage that drove her to insanity.

Closer and closer she came to that glimmering edge. On her every downstroke, he thrust up, and it was so lovely she wanted to cry from its messy perfection. Then her endurance began to flag, but she shouldn't have worried, for he was attuned to every change.

"Let me send you flying, love." His body tensed. He wrapped his legs about hers, tugged her body over his, and then flipped them both over. The emotions shadowing his intense ice blue eyes stole her breath away, but it was the wicked grin that curved his lips and the playful flick of his hips that once more joined them that made her fall all over again. "I can't wait until you are legally mine."

A shiver went down her spine. "Me either." Then she looped her arms about his wide shoulders. "Love me, Hudson."

He nuzzled the skin at the crook of her shoulder. "I believe I have done nothing else since the moment we met." As he moved within her, with slow, shallow strokes, she was lost.

Over and over, their bodies came together. She matched the rhythm he set as if they'd been together for years. When she peeked into his eyes, there was no doubt to the depths of his feelings, for she saw them there in those blue pools, and what was more, she had a glimpse of their future, and it was as beautiful as the man himself.

Tears gathered in her eyes, for she'd often wondered if she could ever love a man the way she had Nathaniel, and while it was true she could, that love was as different as the men themselves. She gasped when Hudson's thrusting changed, became more urgent. Deeper, faster, harder he moved, and each time they came together, frissons of pleasure fractured through her person. "Oh yes, hurry. More, more…"

He grunted in response, but the feel of his strong arms around her, the connection—both physical and emotional—they shared all worked to toss her over the edge into bliss. And he gave her everything that he was, went deeper than she thought possible, with hard, sure strokes that had her eyes crossing.

Seconds later, the feeling of flying assailed her as a second wave of release caught her up in its storm. A keening cry of satisfaction filled the air, and she didn't care if his neighbors heard it, for that was what love was. Loud, messy, scattered, emotional—everything. One stroke then another came from Hudson before he joined her in that flight, and when he collapsed on top of her, she wrapped her arms around him and held him close while his member pulsed into her fluttering core.

As much as she enjoyed the raw closeness that intercourse brought, she adored even more once again having a man to hold, being safe in someone's embrace, feeling content, secure, connected. Tears slipped to her cheeks, for apparently happiness couldn't be contained, and the release wasn't merely just a physical endeavor.

Eventually, her breathing returned to normal, and she came back to earth. While they lay together, she peered beneath the settee only to find that Luna the cat was staring back at her. "Hullo, sweet girl," she crooned to the feline. Would she need to fight with the feline for Hudson's affections and attentions?

The cat merely blinked with her front paws tucked beneath her.

Slowly, so as not to startle the animal, Theodosia reached out a hand, waggled her fingers. "Might we be friends? I adore your owner as much as you do."

When Hudson chuckled, the cat unbent herself enough to sniff at her fingers, then there was the tiniest most fleeting of licks to a fingertip before she retreated further beneath that piece of furniture.

It was a start.

"She doesn't even tolerate Mrs. Claudian that much, so you are already ahead." He rolled them to their sides, kissed her neck, nuzzled the crook of her shoulder, but that only served to fan the smoldering embers in her blood into flames once more.

A sigh escaped her. "I love you." Really, there was nothing else to say.

"I love you, too." He brushed his lips over hers. "Now and always. I can't wait to know your son better, to dare to be a father."

Her heart trembled. "I never thought I would have a husband and a family again, but you have proved me wrong."

"Perhaps we have both rescued each other."

"Yes." Snuggling further into his embrace, she couldn't help but sigh. "Nathaniel's necklace might have saved my life, but you were the one who made me start living it again."

It was funny how fate worked, and she couldn't be happier.

Epilogue

August 15, 1818
Outside a little no-name village in the hills of
Tuscany

Theodosia lifted her head to the breeze as she stood on the balcony just off the room they used for a bedchamber. Rain was in the offing soon, she could smell it, but for now, she intended to enjoy the sunlight while they had it.

She and Hudson had been married for two months and were now enjoying their honeymoon at a villa in the countryside that Thomas had secured through his connections. The trip would be over all too soon and had been quite lovely. Though she missed Jacob, she knew he was probably having a wonderful time in Rome with his uncle, and her brother had no doubt promised the child all sorts of treats and gifts. The boy, bless his soul, had written nearly every day, detailing life with his friends and the adventures he'd found in the courtyard, and almost all of those missives contained questions about Hudson.

It seemed the former Bow Street man had made quite the impression on her son.

"Darling, will you come out here?"

The tunic-style gown she wore of a cheerful yellow silk slid over her skin like a lover's caress. Shivers of anticipation danced down her spine, for she well knew what would happen once her husband caught sight of her dressed like a Roman goddess. Doris had piled her hair high atop her head, loosely securing it with pins. A golden-and-pearl tiara sat upon the tresses while ropes of the same looped about her throat and wrists. Her feet were bare, for she'd gone without footwear was much as she could during this trip.

Here, in the Tuscan countryside, there were no rules.

"Is all well?" He came onto the balcony dressed in tan breeches and a loose-fitting linen shirt that had been rolled up to the elbows.

"It is. I merely wished to see you." She rested a shoulder against a wooden pillar, and with one hand slightly raised the hem of her gown so the side slit in the fabric would show an enticing section of her leg. Hudson had a weakness for them. "What have you got there?"

An ivory envelope was clutched in his hand, but he raked his gaze up and down her body with such slow scrutiny she could have sworn he caressed her. The appreciation in his ice blue eyes never failed to send awareness of him scurrying over her skin. "I heard back from an orphanage in Rome." He waved the letter. "However, I am still waiting on a response from the one you selected in London."

"And?" Flutters went through Theodosia's belly as her heartbeat accelerated. Seeing her husband wasn't the only reason she was excited.

Happiness danced in his eyes. The joy that lined his expression took at least five years from his face. "There is a six-month-old girl available. She is ours once we come in for the interview with the head mistress and leave payment."

It was happening! There was a baby for her! "Is that all?" Scarcely could she believe their good fortune.

"Her name is Lillianna, but I'm thinking we might just call her Lily."

"Yes, of course." She nodded and came a few steps closer to him. "And?"

Though he knew she didn't like to have the anticipation drawn out, he often teased her with it anyway. Today was no exception. "The head mistress says she is of sweet disposition with a bit of sass when she wants. Lily has brown hair that hangs in ringlets and blue eyes like the Roman skies." He cocked an eyebrow. "So? What should we do?"

As if he needed to ask. "I wish to adopt her if you do." A child together of their own. "If you are ready for this next step."

"I am." He struggled with his emotions as he always did, but then, married life and everything that came with it was new to him. "I honestly can't wait to hear someone call me papa; it has long been a dream." With a shake of his head, he looked at her with shock in his gaze. "Please don't misunderstand. I adore Jacob, love being a father to him, can't wait to see how he matures and changes as he grows. I will never replace his own, but I rather doubt he'll call me papa."

"I know. Darling, I know." It felt as if her heart would burst from love. She ran to him, closed the distance, and the second his arms came around her, she pressed fervent kisses to his jaw, his cheeks, his lips. "You have made me so happy, have changed my life, and now we will have a child together."

Oh, it was surely the best day!

"Let us hope I will always remain in your good graces and never disappoint you."

She traced the scars on his cheek. "That won't be possible, for you are you."

"Ah, my sweet Dia." He kissed her soundly then swept her into his arms and carried her into the bedroom.

A sigh escaped her as she gave herself over into his tender and quite insistent care.

Life only needed one little spark and shock to change its direction for the better. The trick was not being afraid of that change. Fate often knew when a person required a bit of a push.

The End

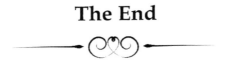

If you enjoyed this book, please leave a review on the site of your choice.

And if you wish to continue reading about the adventures and loves of the other Diamonds of London, go ahead and preorder the next book. More will be coming throughout this year and the next!

The Lady's Daring Gambit (Diamonds of London #2)

Catch Her if You Can (Diamonds of London #3)

Spaghetti with Oil and Garlic (Aglio e Olio)

This is a dish I make at home regularly. It's so easy and usually cheap if you already have the ingredients, and more importantly, my husband eats it without complaint. Since there are so little ingredients, make sure what you do use is top quality. It's not exactly the pasta Hudson and Theodosia ate in this book, but it's close.

Ingredients

Kosher salt
1 pound of spaghetti (or thin spaghetti or linguine noodles)
1 head of garlic, sliced into thin chips (organic)
1/3 cup extra virgin olive oil (the good stuff)
1/3 cup butter (I use organic)
2 tablespoons fresh chopped parsley OR 1 teaspoon dried
1 teaspoon dried crushed red pepper flakes (or less to taste)
1/2 cup freshly grated Parmesan cheese (or grated from the grocery store but make sure it's the good stuff, not from the green can)

Directions

Bring a large pot of cold water to a boil over high heat, then salt generously. (Meaning add at least two tablespoons to the water. You want it to taste like the sea)

Add the pasta and cook, stirring occasionally until al dente, tender but not mushy, about 8 minutes.

While the pasta cooks, combine the garlic, olive oil, butter, and the red pepper flakes in a large skillet and warm over low heat, stirring occasionally, until the garlic softens and turns golden, about 8 minutes.

Very important! Don't let the garlic burn. Otherwise, it will be bitter, and you'll have to start over. I pull it as soon as the garlic is starting to get golden.

Drain the pasta in a colander set in the sink.

Add the pasta to the garlic mixture. Mix well.

Add the parsley.

Adjust seasoning, to taste. Meaning add a tiny bit of salt if needed.

Transfer to a large serving bowl or divide amongst 4 to 6 dishes. Serve topped with grated cheese.

You could also add a sprinkling of lemon zest here if you'd like.

Regency-era romances by Sandra Sookoo

Willful Winterbournes series

Romancing Miss Quill
Pursuing Mr. Mattingly
Courting Lady Yeardly
Teasing Miss Atherby
Guarding the Widow Pellingham (coming May 2023)
Bedeviling Major Kenton (coming August 2023)
Charming Miss Standish (coming November 2023)

Singular Sensation series

One Little Indiscretion
One Secret Wish
One Tiny On Dit Later
Duchess of Moonlight
One Accidental Night with an Improper Duke (coming April 2023)
One Scandalous Choice (coming July 2023)
One Thing Led to Another (coming October 2023)
One Suitor Too Many (coming January 2024)
One of a Kind (as part of the *Gentleman and Gloves* anthology
coming February 2024)
One Track Mind (coming April 2024)
One Night in Covent Garden (coming August 2024)
One Christmas Disaster (coming December 2024)

Mary and Bright mystery series

An Affair at Christmastide (coming December 2023)
An Intriguing Springtime Engagement (coming April 2024)
Autumn Means Marriage… and Murder (coming October 2024)

Diamonds of London series

My Dear Mr. Ridley
The Lady's Daring Gambit (coming June 2023)
Catch Her if You Can (coming September 2023)
Magic for Christmas (coming December 2023)
When the Duke Said Yes (coming February 2024)
Along Came Tess (coming June 2024)
A Ghostly Affair (coming September 2024)
Spending Christmas in Hell (coming November 2024)
The Duke's Accidental Mistress (coming January 2025)
Only Spring will Do (coming April 2025)
Not His Usual Style (coming May 2025)
The Duchess Problem (coming July 2025)
The Recalcitrant Lady (coming October 2025)
A Bit of Christmas Fiction (coming November 2025)
If a Spinster Wishes (coming January 2026)

Hasting Sisters

The Devil's Game (coming March 2024)
A Second Summertime Courtship (coming May 2024)
An Impossible Match (coming July 2024)

Disreputable Dukes of Club Damnation

Ravenhurst's Return (coming November 2024)
His by Sunrise (coming February 2025)
Promised to the Worst Duke in England (coming April 2025)
The Devil's in the Details (coming July 2025)
The Duchess' Damning Letters (coming August 2025)
Buckthorne's Secret (coming October 2025)
A Duchess for Christmas (coming December 2025)
Pursuing the Duke of Hearts (coming February 2026)
In Hell by Default (coming April 2026)
To Woo a Duke (coming June 2026)
Three Nights with the Devil (coming August 2026)
To Hell with the Duchess (coming October 2026)

Boxers of Brook Street

With Love in Their Corner (coming March 2025)
Go Down Swinging for Love (coming June 2025)
On the Ropes of Scandal (September 2025)